DEEP SECRETS

Illustrator Gemma has made a new life for herself in London, far away from her quiet childhood home in Westlea Bay. But shortly after her best friend Penny moves to the city to live with her boyfriend Brian, the couple disappear — and all clues seem to point back to the seaside town where the two friends grew up. Arriving at the missing pair's home shortly after Gemma, Brian's brother Dan is also drawn into the mystery. Can the two of them solve it — or is Dan hiding something too?

ENID REECE

DEEP SECRETS

Complete and Unabridged

LINFORD
Leicester

First published in Great Britain in 2018

First Linford Edition
published 2020

A catalogue record for this book is available
from the British Library.

ISBN 978–1–4448–4432–0

Published by
Ulverscroft Limited
Anstey, Leicestershire

Set by Words & Graphics Ltd.
Anstey, Leicestershire
Printed and bound in Great Britain by
T. J. International Ltd., Padstow, Cornwall

This book is printed on acid-free paper

1

'Oh, please come,' Penny said. 'It's been such a long time.'

Gemma sighed and rubbed tired eyes. 'Oh Penny, I'm not sure. I've a commission I need to finish and I'm on a deadline.'

'Surely you could spare just one weekend from your busy schedule, Gemma? I've been nagging you since I arrived in London and all you've given me is excuses. Come on, it'll be fun.'

Gemma detected a plea in her friend's voice and felt a pang of guilt. It was true. Every time in the last few weeks when Penny rang to arrange a meet up, she'd put her off. She missed her best friend since she moved from her home town of Westlea Bay. Now, 18 months later, Penny had followed her to London.

'OK, I'll come. Are you sure I can

stay over? Brian all right with it?'

'Of course. Brian was the one who suggested it. Just think of the fantastic time we'll have. I already feel homesick. Who would have thought I'd miss sleepy Westlea Bay and all our favourite places? The beach, the pier, the folly. Oh, Gem, I've missed you so much.'

'Me too. Look, I have to go. I'll text you my ETA in the morning.'

Saying goodbye, Gemma turned off her mobile. Moving to London had been a big step for her. Westlea Bay, the little seaside town on the Sussex coast had been her home for the first 25 years of her life and it would have stayed that way if it hadn't been for Robbie the Rat. She shook off the invasion of that thought, he wasn't worth a moment of her precious time. She thought back to her conversation with Penny. She frowned, sure that she'd missed something in the conversation but it was snatched away before she could grip onto it. Oh well, it would come to her eventually.

★ ★ ★

Two days later and an uneasy feeling crept over Gemma as she stood outside the home of her best friend. The front door was open, not fully, just slightly ajar. She gave it a nudge and stepped inside the hallway closing the door behind her.

'Penny?' Silence.

Where was she?

She walked further along the hallway, the only sound her feet treading the wooden flooring. Peering into the kitchen she saw a couple of mugs in the sink, the remains of a meal on the table. Shards of broken crockery lay on the floor. Gemma frowned. It was unlike Penny to leave an untidy kitchen.

Gemma moved into the main living area. A couple of magazines lay scattered on the floor. Slipped off the coffee table? Penny wasn't sure. Books were dislodged on the bookcase as though someone hadn't pushed them

3

back into place. A wastepaper basket was on its side, a few pieces of scrunched up paper straightened out then tossed aside. Everything could be explained but Gemma felt some niggle of doubt creep through her. This was not Penny at all.

Gemma called out again but there was nothing. Perhaps she was ill? She climbed the stairs. Discovering the main bedroom, there was no Penny, only an unmade bed. The wardrobe door was open, clothes and coat hangers scattered on the floor. She frowned and pulled her phone out of her pocket, dialling Penny's number. Hearing the sound of a phone ringing from downstairs she retraced her steps. The bright pink mobile was pushed down between the cushions of the settee. Her friend never went anywhere without it.

Placing it onto the coffee table she sank into the sofa and closed her eyes, wondering what was happening.

At the sound of a key turning in the

4

front door, Gemma relaxed. Penny was home.

She turned to greet her friend only to be surprised to see a man of about 30, tall with dark hair and an impressive amount of stubble around his face, standing in the doorway, a travel case in one hand, the other resting on one lean hip. Piercing blue eyes looked her up and down.

'Who are you?' She kept her voice steady, trying not to show how unsettled she felt. It wasn't Brian. This man was a stranger. An imposing stranger. She looked around the room to see if there was anything she could defend herself with.

'Penny, I assume?' he said, raising an enquiring eyebrow before stepping further into the room and putting his bag on the floor.

Gemma gulped at the sight before her, breathing a sigh of relief. He knew Penny. Was that a good or bad thing?

'Sorry, no. I'm Gemma, Penny's best friend. I've only just arrived. Penny invited me for the weekend but she's not here and the door was open and then I found all this mess.' Running out of steam, Gemma stopped. 'And you?'

He scrubbed a hand over the bristle on his chin. 'I'm Dan, Brian's brother.'

Gemma relaxed a little. She knew Brian had a brother, a travel writer who often worked away.

'I've just flown into Heathrow,' he continued. 'Where's Brian? He knew I was coming home today. He must have forgotten . . .'

'No idea,' said Gemma. 'Penny appears to be missing as well.'

'Hang on, let me give him a call,' he said, digging out his mobile from his trouser pocket and dialling. He shook his head. 'Straight to answer,' he said after a moment.

Gemma rose from the sofa. 'There must be a logical reason,' she said, running a hand through her hair.

'You're right, there has to be an explanation. They'll both turn up soon with some excuse or other. Look, I don't know about you but I could do with a strong cup of coffee.' He gave her a reassuring smile and headed towards the kitchen. 'Travelling for two days can be pretty tiring.'

The smile changed his whole demeanour. One minute he appeared threatening, the next — well, Gemma wasn't certain. She pushed away wayward thoughts and turned her mind to her missing friend.

'Not much of a housekeeper your mate, Penny,' he said, looking around the untidy kitchen.

'That's another odd thing. Penny is one of the tidiest people I've ever met. Everything has a place. It's not like her to leave a mess like this. She would have, at least, loaded the dishwasher. Brian's the same. One of the things Penny liked about him.'

Dan nodded and began making the coffee with quick efficiency. He really was good looking, thought Gemma.

'I'll clear these away,' she said, unable to do nothing. She began collecting dirty dishes while Dan busied himself making the coffee. She caught a whiff of his woody aftershave. Too aware of his closeness she moved away to sit at the kitchen table.

'You know,' he said, curling slim fingers around the mugs and offering her one before settling down on a chair opposite her, 'I think they may have left in a hurry.'

'Oh,' Gemma frowned, trying to think of anything that would make sense. 'Perhaps they've gone shopping.'

'Wouldn't she have rung to tell you?' said Dan, taking a sip of coffee.

'I found her phone in the living room, pushed down the side of the sofa. She never goes anywhere without it.'

'Neither does Brian. Let's hope he'll return my call soon.'

'What makes you think they left in a hurry?' said Gemma, running a finger along the rim of her mug.

'The broken crockery.' He stood up, pulled a dustpan and brush from under the sink, sweeping up the shattered pieces. 'For two very tidy people they would have cleaned up before they left. And another thing, for a couple expecting visitors for the weekend there is very little in the fridge.' He emptied the dustpan in the bin and opened the fridge door.

Gemma peered over his shoulder. A carton of milk, a couple of bottles of water and a piece of cheese that looked well past its sell by date.

'You know, none of this adds up. Penny is so organised. This is so not her.' Gemma chewed at her lip. 'We should ring the hospitals. See if there's been an accident.'

Dan hesitated for a moment, looking concerned.

'And perhaps the police,' she added trying to empathise the worry she felt about the situation.

Dan scrubbed a hand over his face and nodded. 'OK. Look, you ring the hospitals and I'll ring the police, although I'm not sure what they will do. We've got nothing concrete to tell them, only our suspicions that some-thing may have happened to Brian and Penny.'

Gemma sighed with relief. 'But at least we'll be doing something.'

'There's a list of the nearest hospitals on the noticeboard.' He nodded towards the wall behind her. 'I'll just put my bag in my bedroom and then I'll phone the police.'

Detecting the worried look on his face as he walked past didn't give her much relief.

⋆   ⋆   ⋆

'Any luck?' said Dan, walking into the kitchen 10 minutes later.

Gemma shook her head. 'Nothing. You?'

'I've made a missing person's report. They'll act on it if we don't hear anything after 48 hours. They'll need a picture of them both. I've got one of Brian but not Penny. In fact, I have no idea what she looks like. I've been travelling during their whirlwind romance. Brian only emailed a month ago that they'd moved in together.'

'No worries, I have a picture of them both that Penny sent me. Here, it's on my phone.'

She scrolled through her phone until she found what she was looking for. Brian and Penny were standing against the backdrop of the sandy beach of home, their arms wrapped around each other and laughing into the camera.

'Pretty girl,' commented Dan, as Gemma held up the picture for his perusal. 'Send it to my phone and I'll email it to the police.' Giving her his mobile number, Gemma tapped it into her mobile and sent the picture.

'So what do we do now?' she said.

'Well, I don't know about you but I'm going to get something to eat.'

'Eat? Shouldn't we be doing something?' Gemma wasn't sure she could eat a thing. Worrying about Penny was all she could think about at the moment.

Dan shrugged. 'Like what?'

Gemma pushed a hand through her hair trying to hold back her frustration. 'Well, I don't know. Check if the neighbours have seen them. Walk around a bit. We might find them.'

'Walk around a bit? Do you know how big London is?' he said, looking at her in amazement.

'Of course. I know how big London is,' she said, a little irritated by his comment.

'OK,' said Dan, putting his hands up. 'I'll check with the neighbours but I'm not walking around the streets of London, late at night, just on the off chance that I bump into my brother and his girlfriend.'

Gemma could see the sense of what he was saying. It was ridiculous to think that walking the street would find her friend. 'OK,' she said.

He gave her a reassuring smile. 'We'll find them, Gemma. Try not to worry.'

She gave a nervous laugh just as her stomach rumbled, reminding her that she hadn't eaten since lunch time.

He reached into a drawer and pulled out a menu. 'Hope you like pizza? How about you order for us both and I'll go and check with the neighbours. Plenty of cheese and pepperoni for me,' he said before heading out of the kitchen.

The neighbours were no help at all. They were at work all day and very rarely saw Brian or Gemma.

'One thing I did check, though. Brian's car. It's not in its usual parking spot. So wherever they went they're using the car,' said Dan as he pushed his plate aside half an hour later.

'Is that a good or bad thing?' said Gemma, putting aside the remainder of her pizza and wiping her hands on a napkin.

Dan frowned. 'I'm not sure. Brian very rarely uses it when at home. Parking is an issue so the only time he usually drives is for the supermarket run. Any other time he takes the tube.'

'So they must have gone out of London?'

'Looks like it. I'll give the registration to the police. Hopefully they'll be able to trace it quickly.'

He stifled a yawn. 'Sorry, can't seem to keep my eyes open.'

Gemma checked her watch. 'It's late. Not sure I fancy catching the train to the other side of London at this time of the day.'

'Stay the night,' he said.

'Pardon,' she said, surprised at his suggestion.

'Look, you were planning to anyway, so why not? There's another bedroom that doubles up as a study. There's a futon in there. It's comfy.'

She thought for a moment before making a decision. 'OK, if you're sure.'

'Positive. Look, I'm heading for bed. Sorry to be a killjoy but I'm almost sleeping on my feet here. We'll talk in the morning. Sort this mess out. OK?'

Gemma nodded in agreement.

'Night, Dan, sleep tight,' she said, as he climbed the stairs.

He turned and gave her a warm

smile. 'It will be OK, I promise. I'll leave some bedding out for you. Bedroom's top of the stairs, first on the right. Night, Gemma.'

Gemma sat for a while and went over everything that had happened. Her eyelids felt heavy. It had been a long day and everything was jumbled up in her mind. A good night's sleep and all would become clear. The light was off in Dan's bedroom and she could hear gentle snores — exhaustion must have taken over quickly. She smiled as she prepared herself for bed. There was no doubt in her mind that he would sort out all the confusion in the morning. He just had that air of confidence about him. She pulled back the duvet and climbed into bed. Within minutes she was asleep.

⋆   ⋆   ⋆

The smell of coffee roused Gemma. She stretched and opened her eyes, wondering at first where she was until

15

she recalled the events of the previous evening. She could hear noises and quickly put on her dressing gown.

'Morning,' said Dan as she walked into the warm kitchen.

He'd showered, his hair still damp and the scruff of a beard had disappeared. Shame, she thought, she rather liked a man with stubble.

'Coffee?' He held up a mug and she nodded her thanks.

She sat down at the table and swept a lock of ash blonde hair away from her face.

'I popped to the shop on the corner and bought a few provisions for breakfast,' he said.

She watched him expertly crack an egg into the frying pan with one hand while popping a piece of bread into the toaster with the other. A man used to fending for himself. She was liking him more.

Half an hour later, Gemma scraped the last piece of egg off her plate and leaned back.

'Think I've gained a stone,' she said, rubbing her tummy.

Dan studied her for a moment. 'No way, you're just right. Can't stand skinny women.'

'Thanks, I think,' she said, wiping her mouth with her napkin before scrunching it up and tossing it onto her empty plate.

He turned a slight shade of pink. 'Sorry, I didn't mean to imply there was anything wrong with you.'

'I'll forgive you, this time,' she said, giving him a teasing grin.

A comfortable silence settled between them as both became lost in their own thoughts.

'You know, I've been thinking, maybe it would be a good idea if you went home and I sorted this mess out myself.'

Gemma sat up in her chair, her back rigid. 'No way, I'm seeing this through till the end. How could you possibly think I would want to do anything else?' Her voice rose, her anger clearly

17

displayed by the redness in her face.

Dan held up his hands in defence. 'Sorry, I just thought it would be easier on you, that's all. Maybe safer.'

'You don't have to worry about me, Dan. I'll be fine.' She said nothing for a moment, trying to calm her temper and let his words sink in. 'What do you mean 'safer'?'

Dan shrugged. 'Nothing really. I don't doubt for a minute that they are both fine. But something could have happened to them.'

'We should have checked the hospitals again.'

'I did that this morning — nothing. Sorry, Gemma, forgot to mention it.'

Gemma felt a little hurt that he hadn't shared that little piece of information with her but decided to let it go for the moment. She watched him drumming his fingers on the table as if trying to decide something. The tapping stopped and he looked at her.

'When you last spoke to Penny was there anything out of the ordinary?'

'No. I don't think so.' Gemma frowned, trying to think of something. 'She was excited about me coming to see her. Almost pleading now I come to think about it.'

'Nothing else come to mind?'

A memory popped into her head. 'Well, I suppose there was one thing.' She shook her head. 'No, it's nothing really.'

'Go on, it might be important.'

'She mentioned the folly.'

'The folly?' Dan gave her a puzzled look.

'Westlea folly. It's a Victorian buildings from the nineteenth century.'

She lifted her coffee mug and drained the last of the liquid.

'So what was off about that?' Dan prompted.

'Well, I suppose it's nothing really. Just that she said next time she came home she wanted to go and see it since it was one of our favourite childhood haunts.'

'What's off about that?' asked Dan,

19

giving her a puzzled look.

'Well, that's just it — it wasn't.'

Dan sighed. 'Wasn't what?'

'Sorry, I'm not getting to the point. Look, it was never a favourite of Penny's.' It wasn't one of Gemma's either but she wasn't going to admit that. 'She was never keen on it, thought it a bit creepy, plus she didn't have a head for heights.'

'Why would that bother her?' Dan asked.

'The folly is built overlooking the bay. Over the years the cliffs have eroded and the folly is slowly getting nearer the sea. As kids, we used to dare each other to creep up to the edge and see the rocks below. Penny hated doing it but she did it all the same.' Gemma didn't admit that their dare devil games had given her nightmares as a child. She shuddered at the thought.

Before Dan could respond his mobile rang.

'Is it Brian?' Gemma crossed her fingers.

Dan shook his head, 'Sorry, no. Work. Look I'll take it in my room, won't be a minute.'

'Sorry about that,' he said, returning after a couple of minutes. 'The magazine wants to know how long before I send in my copy.' He poured himself another coffee. 'I've been thinking, we should head towards your home town.'

'So you think the folly could be a clue? Shouldn't we tell the police?'

'Well, it's only a hunch, so let's see where it leads us.'

Two hours later they were on a train headed towards Westlea Bay.

2

Dan stared at his laptop. He'd turned it on as soon as they'd settled in their seats on the train, explaining to Gemma that he needed to start his article on China for a Sunday supplement. In reality, he needed some space to think. Brian's disappearance was worrying. What had his brother got himself involved in?

China had been a long trip and he'd been looking forward to catching up as they always did when Dan was away for a period of time. Dan just hoped he wasn't in trouble, although it did seem to follow his baby brother around. When they were kids he was always helping out his younger sibling when he got into one scrap after another.

From what Brian had told him, Penny sounded just the right girl for him. Someone to keep his brother on the straight and narrow.

Irritated with himself for worrying too much about his brother, he turned his attention back to his laptop. He needed to get on with the article. Putting on his reading glasses, he pulled up his notes and was soon lost in the beauty of China.

'Ham and tomato or cheese and pickle?'

Engrossed in his work he hadn't seen Gemma leave her seat and go to the refreshment area.

'Whatever, I don't mind,' he murmured, not looking up.

She pushed the cheese and pickle towards him before reaching into her bag and pulling out two bottles of water, passing one to him.

''Thanks' would be good,' she said.

Detecting sarcasm in her voice Dan looked up and gave her an apologetic smile.

'Sorry. When I start an article I get so carried away. I notice nothing around me.'

23

Gemma nodded and picked up the magazine she'd bought before they got on the train.

'I'll let you get on with it then,' she said and began flipping through the pages.

He watched her for a moment. Her blonde hair hung loose around her face and for a brief moment he wondered what it would be like to run his fingers through the glossy strands.

He brushed the thought from his mind, annoyed with himself. He had no time for romance.

Gemma looked up suddenly and their eyes met. She raised an eyebrow and he knew he'd been caught staring. He said nothing, just turned his attention back to his laptop.

Another hour passed and his stomach began to rumble. His sandwich was still by his side, untouched. He pulled it out of its wrapping and took a healthy bite. He looked over at Gemma. She'd pulled out a notebook from her bag and was sketching a portrait. The likeness was good, he thought, as he recognised Penny. A few more swift strokes and the picture was finished.

'You're very good,' he said, nodding towards the sketch.

'Thanks. I do it for a living.'

'What, portraits?' He couldn't keep the surprise out of his voice. She didn't come across as someone who painted all day.

'No, I'm an illustrator — for cards.'

He frowned, not sure what she meant.

'Birthday, anniversary cards. Stuff like that.'

'Interesting work,' he said before turning his attention back to his laptop.

Half an hour later he pulled his glasses off his nose and rubbed tired eyes. He checked his watch. Not long now and they would be there.

'Can you recommend anywhere I can stay?' he asked, turning his attention to Gemma.

'The Ship — it's on the seafront and at this time of year it's quiet. The season's over so I'm sure they'll be glad of the custom. I know the owner so you'll be OK.'

'Perfect. Will you be staying there as well?'

Gemma shook her head.

'No. I rang my mother before we left.' She frowned. 'Sorry they can't put you up, although I suppose at a push you could sleep on the sofa.'

'No apologies needed. The Ship sounds fine.'

'Do you think we'll find the answers we're looking for?' she asked, chewing her bottom lip.

'I hope so,' he said. 'Where should we start? The folly?'

Gemma shook her head. 'No, I think it's best if we visit Penny's dad. He may have heard from her, although I doubt it.'

'Really? Why?'

Gemma shrugged. 'Penny's like me — an only child. Her mum died when she was twelve and she became very close to her dad. They seemed to lean

26

on each other for support.'

'Understandable,' remarked Dan.

'Yes, well all was OK until your brother came on the scene. The new pharmaceutical rep walks into the chemist shop where she works and in an instant they're a couple. Her dad became jealous of the closeness that developed and when she declared that she was off to London there was a big row and they haven't spoken since.'

Dan leant forward. 'Do you think he might have gone to London and done her harm?' To be honest he didn't really think that, but the question had to be asked.

'Definitely not. Sam Tremayne can be a grumpy old man but he'd never hurt her.'

Dan noted a sharpness in her voice but pressed on. 'What about Brian? Would Sam harm him?'

Gemma breathed in sharply and sat up straight. 'No, no. Never. He may be jealous but he isn't a violent man.'

'But there was a row,' Dan pointed

out, ignoring the anger flashing in her eyes.

'True, but I think the problem is that Sam is stubborn and won't admit that he was in the wrong. He'll come round in time, I'm sure.'

Dan relaxed a little.

'So what exactly are you going to say to him?'

Gemma leaned back in her seat. 'I'm not sure. I don't think it's a good idea to mention Penny's disappearance. No good raising the alarm until we hear from the police. Hopefully he's heard from her or knows where she is.'

'Well, fingers crossed he'll have some answers for us.'

She nodded, picked up her magazine again and said nothing further for the rest of the journey.

⋆　⋆　⋆

Dan pushed his ticket into the machine and walked through the turnstile following Gemma out of the station.

The salt air hit his nostrils and he was transported back to summer holidays. Buckets and spades, hours spent on the beach collecting shells with his brother and looking for sea urchins.

The train station was just off the seafront and they headed towards the harbour. Fishing boats were anchored, the daily catch already brought in. A few fishermen sat at the dock repairing nets, and the smell of fish was in the air.

'The Ship is just down here,' said Gemma, stepping up the pace. 'Whitey will welcome you with open arms.'

'Whitey?'

'Joan White, landlady and owner of The Ship since . . . well, since forever.'

'Forever,' Dan smiled, imagining a little old lady with white hair.

'Well, ever since I can remember. Mum and Dad used to take me there for Sunday lunch occasionally as a special treat. You'll love it. Nothing fancy, so if you want something more up-market you will have to move down the coast.'

'Nothing fancy is fine by me,' he said, giving a wry smile.

The outside was painted white, although by the looks of it, the walls could do with a spruce up as there was paint peeling in various places. He stepped into the hotel. Gemma rang the bell at the small reception area in the hallway as Dan took in his surroundings.

The place had a seventies feel to it. Flock nylon wallpaper hung on the walls and a heavily patterned carpet lay on the floor — it could to with a bit of an update but it looked clean.

'Gemma, dearie,' a voice said from behind him and Dan turned round. If this was Whitey, she was nothing like the woman he was expecting. At five foot four, Joan White was nothing like a little old lady. Her hair was a bright shade of red, out of a bottle if Dan wasn't mistaken. Her face was scrubbed clean of any make-up and her green eyes sparkled with humour. Flowing robes covered her body, flip flops covered her feet — Dan tried not to stare. She reminded him of a hippy from the sixties stuck in a time warp.

'Whitey,' exclaimed Gemma, reaching out and giving the woman a hug. 'How are you?'

'I'm fine, dearie. Seems an age since I last saw you.'

'Sorry, I've been home a couple of times since my move but not had time to visit.'

Whitey patted her shoulder. 'No worries, I know what busy lives you youngsters lead.' She turned her head towards Dan and raised an eyebrow.

'Sorry,' said Gemma. 'This is Dan, a friend of mine. He'd like a room if you have one?'

'No problem,' said Whitey, moving the stand behind the little reception desk and pushing the registration book towards Dan. 'Just sign in. There's plenty of vacancies this time of year. I have a nice room overlooking the bay.'

'That will do nicely. Thanks,' said

Dan, picking up a pen and filling in his details.

Whitey handed him a key. 'Top of the stairs, along the corridor to the end. Sorry, no porter to carry your bags. Hope you can manage?'

He turned to Gemma. 'I'll see you soon.'

'Give me an hour to drop my case off at my parents,' she said, 'and I'll meet you back here. We'll take a walk along the harbour.'

'Oh, I thought . . . '

'Just as we discussed,' Gemma interrupted him before he could say anything else.

'OK,' said Dan, wondering why Gemma was being so mysterious about visiting Penny's father?

Gemma nodded before turning to Whitey. 'See you soon. I'll most likely be calling in for a drink while Dan is staying here. We can catch up with all the gossip then.'

'Nice girl,' said Whitey as they both watched Gemma walk out of the door.

Dan nodded in agreement before turning towards the stairs. 'Right, I'd better get settled in or Gemma will be back before I'm ready.'

★   ★   ★

'The shop is just along the front, by the harbour,' said Gemma, an hour later. 'I'll introduce you as a friend.'

'Why not tell him who I am?' said Dan.

'No need to antagonise him. Knowing you're Brian's brother might raise his anger.'

'Wouldn't he know that Brian has a brother already?' he asked, bemused.

'From what Penny told me, Sam didn't get to know him that well. In fact, I think they only met twice, and that was only for a couple of minutes. Not enough time to find out his life history.'

'OK. Another question. Why didn't you want Whitey to know who I was?'

Gemma shrugged. 'No reason. Just

33

think it's better if we keep our search to ourselves for now.'

'Fair enough. Come on, let's see what information we can get from Penny's dad.'

There were no windows showing off any merchandise, just a front door with a sign above reading 'The Tackle Shop' and a sign below stating 'Summer Fishing Trips Available'. Pushing the door open, Gemma heard a bell sound from somewhere inside. The smell offish bait and salt water filled the air. Every kind of fishing tackle was on display on ceiling to floor shelves.

Rods of all sizes were stacked against one wall and a small desk stood in one corner with an old-fashioned cash register on top. There was no sign of Sam Tremayne.

'He must be out back,' said Gemma, walking towards a door at the back of the shop. She saw Sam as soon as she opened the door, sitting on a chair, mending a large net.

'Hi Sam.'

The weather-beaten face looked up. His dark hair, sprinkled with grey framed his head. His thin lips tightened in displeasure perhaps at being disturbed. 'Gemma. Not seen you for a while,' he acknowledged before turning his attention back to his mending.

Gemma looked at Dan and shrugged. It was going to be more difficult than she first thought.

'This is Dan, a friend of mine. He's interested in a fishing trip.'

Penny saw Dan raise an eyebrow and open his mouth to speak. She shook her head, lifting her hand to silence him.

'Finished for the season,' said Sam, looking at Dan for the first time.

'Well, no worries,' interrupted Dan before Penny could speak again. 'I'm only here for a few days anyway.'

Sam said nothing but carried on with his task.

'Oh well, it was worth asking,' said Gemma after a moment, before deciding that she might as well ask about her friend without hesitation.

'Have you heard from Penny at all? I've been so busy myself that I haven't spoken to her for a while, and not since she moved to London.'

'Not a word. Not since she left with that fella.' He sniffed and adjusted the large piece of netting on his lap.

'Still not speaking then?' asked Gemma.

Sam picked up a knife and cut at a piece of netting. 'Nothing to speak about until she comes to her senses.'

Gemma opened her mouth to say something but decided against it. Sam was still hurting and it would do no good to antagonise him.

'Oh well, I'll catch up with her once I return to London. I did ring her before I came home but got no reply. She must have gone away on holiday. Did she mentioned anything to you before she moved out?'

'As if she'd tell me anything.' He held up the netting to insect the repairs before continuing.

'She might have mentioned it to that

girl she worked with. Got quite friendly with her once you left. Always meeting up and going out after work.'

'Do you mean Hayley?' Gemma asked.

'Yep, that's the girl.'

'Oh, right. Well thanks, Sam. We'll let you get on.' Gemma was suddenly in a hurry to leave.

Sam looked up from his net. 'Sorry I can't help with the fishing trip.'

'Another time,' said Dan and followed Gemma out of the shop.

Once outside, Gemma stopped and turned to Dan. 'How odd.'

'Odd. What do you mean?'

'I didn't know that she was friends with Hayley. In fact, I'm sure she wasn't.'

'And you know that, how?'

Gemma bit down on her lip. 'Well, for one thing she would have told me and I just can't imagine she would have anything in common with Hayley.'

Dan raised an eyebrow.

She continued. 'Their age difference

for a start. Hayley was just out of school, working in the chemist shop was her first job.'

'Perhaps she was missing you, her best friend, and reached out to the nearest person at hand.'

'Maybe, but that doesn't explain why Penny hasn't mention it to me.'

'Perhaps she thought you'd be jealous?'

Gemma shook her head. 'No, that's not it. Penny would know that I wouldn't get jealous.'

She brushed a strand of hair away from her forehead. 'Look, it's been a long day. I'm going to head home. I'll meet you in the morning. We'll go up to the folly, see if we can find out anything. Then I think a visit to Hayley is a good idea. Hopefully she can tell us how friendly she was with Penny.'

Dan rubbed a hand over his five o'clock shadow. 'Not a bad idea.'

It was dark now. They stopped to look out onto the expanse of water in front of them. A full moon shone down from a cloudless night. Lights from a ship anchored out in the distance looked like small dots on the horizon.

Penny gave a sigh of satisfaction. 'I love this time of the year. The peace and quiet. I miss it.' She looked at Dan. He said nothing, just continued looking out at the waves. Worry lines formed on his brow and she knew he was thinking about his brother. She reached for his hand and gave it a gentle squeeze. Dark eyes looked into hers and for one moment she thought he was going to kiss her.

The sound of his mobile going off interrupted whatever was going to happen and he pulled away, reaching for his phone.

'Is it . . . ?' she asked, her hopes rising.

He shook his head. 'Sorry. It's work. I have to take it.'

He walked off out of hearing distance and Gemma looked out to sea once more. The lights from the ship were flashing. A warning to other shipping she thought, although something about the movement of the lights didn't seem quite right. She heard footsteps behind her. Turning, she forgot about what she'd just seen.

'Everything OK?' she asked.

He nodded and pushed a hand through his hair. 'Fine, just my editor wanting to know when my article will be finished. You're right, we should both get an early night. I'm still trying to get over jet lag. Another early night and I should be OK. I'll walk you home first.'

'Oh, it's OK. My parents live at the other end of the bay. I'll be fine.'

'You're sure?'

'Positive,' she said. If she was being honest with herself she could do with a little time by herself. The last 24 hours were catching up with her. There were too many thoughts going around in her head and she needed to sort them all out. The best way to do that was on her own. With a wave he said goodnight and she watched him walk along the seafront, his hands deep in his pockets and his head down. She was beginning to trust him and that worried her.

3

A fresh breeze hung in the air as Gemma made her way along the seafront. There was still no word from Penny. Gemma had left another message on her voicemail and after checking her phone at least three times she'd given up. Hopefully Dan had had more luck with his brother.

She still wasn't sure about Brian. There had been something Dan was holding back about his sibling. Nothing definite she could pin down. Just a feeling gnawing at her. She could ask Dan but after only knowing each other for two days, she doubted he would confide in her.

It wasn't quite nine o'clock so she stopped by the dock, watching a couple of sail boats. There was a larger vessel anchored out on the horizon, reminding her of the flashing lights of the night before. A ship with problems, maybe? She pushed a lock of windswept hair behind her ear and with one last look walked away.

*   *   *

Dan was nowhere to be seen when she entered the pub but Whitey was just clearing a table of breakfast dishes. She looked up as Gemma entered and gave her a smile.

'Morning, dearie. You waiting for your young man?' she called out.

'If you mean my friend Dan, then yes,' said Gemma, trying to keep the irritation out of her voice. Why did people assume that a man and woman couldn't just be friends? If Whitey sensed anything wrong she chose to take no notice.

'He's just popped up to his room for a jacket. I told him there was a swell out to sea and he might need wrapping up. See you thought the same.' She nodded to the tan leather jacket that Gemma had matched up with a soft blue sweater and jeans. Blue pumps finished off the outfit.

Before Gemma could reply Dan appeared, mobile phone in one hand, a grey jacket slung over his shoulder, a pale lemon polo shirt emphasising a flat stomach and muscled arms. Jeans hugged his long legs. He looked good.

'Morning,' said Gemma, feeling a blush creeping onto her face. She'd been staring again and the slight upturn of Dan's lips suggested he knew exactly what effect he had on her. 'Ready to go?'

'Ready as I'll ever be. See you later, Whitey,' he said, tucking his mobile into his pocket before holding the door open for Gemma.

Gemma caught a whiff of woody aftershave. For heaven's sake, even his cologne was attractive.

She shook thoughts of Dan's masculinity out of her head, gave Whitey a wave and headed out into the street, Dan following behind her.

'Hope you've got your walking legs on today,' said Gemma as they headed along to the promenade. 'The folly is a bit of a distance and it's uphill. Just beyond those cliffs over there.' She pointed in the direction they were heading. 'Luckily there's a footpath, although it can be a bit rocky in places.'

'Hey, I'll have you know these legs have walked a good distance along the Great Wall of China. A small hill is nothing.'

Gemma chuckled. 'OK, I believe you. Come on, let's get going.'

'Heard anything from Brian this morning?' she asked as they left the promenade behind and began climbing the uphill slope of the pathway.

'Nothing. How about Penny?'

She shook her head. 'Not a word.'

The higher they climbed, the stronger the wind became. Dan shrugged on his jacket and Gemma tied back her hair with an elastic band she produced from her pocket. They stopped for a moment to gaze out over the bay. The

45

weather was holding onto a late summer, bringing a few visitors to the beach. There were even a few brave bathers attempting a dip in the sea. Further out on the water there were a couple of jet skis cutting through the waves leaving a trail of white foam behind them.

'Ever tried it?' he asked, nodding towards the jet skiers.

'A couple of times,' admitted Gemma. 'Believe it or not I get sea sick.' Seeing the look on his face she laughed. 'I know it sounds stupid growing up in a coastal town.' She shook her head. 'Although that doesn't mean I don't try to overcome the problem. Just don't try inviting me on a six month cruise any time soon.'

Dan grinned and leaned forward. 'Don't tell anyone but I suffer from air sickness.'

'No,' said Gemma, amazed at his admission.

'It's true,' he said, his eyes sparkling with merriment. 'I'm OK once I'm in the air but the up and the down bit makes my stomach roll over. Not pleasant at all.'

'Oh no, not good for a travel writer. We make a good pair. Just imagine arranging a holiday together. We'd have to go by train!' She shut her mouth, suddenly realising what she'd said. Where on earth had the words 'holiday together' come from? She turned back towards the footpath. 'Come on, another five minutes and we should be there.'

Dan followed, not saying a word for which she was thankful.

'There's a gate up ahead,' she said, breaking the silence. 'It leads into a field. At the far end there's a small copse. The folly is just in front.'

'I can see why this would be heaven for a child,' said Dan. 'I can just imagine you and Penny scampering among the trees, playing hide and seek. I'll bet you even climbed a few.'

'Heaven's the right word,' said Penny, her eyes bright with excitement as she opened the gate. She began to run to her old playground only to stop in her tracks as the folly came into view.

'Goodness,' said Dan. 'It's a mini replica of the Dome of St Paul's Cathedral.'

'Impressive, isn't it?' remarked Gemma.

'It certainly is.'

'Oh no,' she exclaimed as they walked nearer.

Rolls of barbed wire and a large 'KEEP OUT' sign prevented them going any further.

Dan read aloud the rest of the sign, 'Danger, building in state of collapse.' He sighed. 'It doesn't look that bad to me,' he said, leaning in towards the barbed wire, trying to get a better view of the building.

'Be careful, Dan,' advised Gemma, keeping well back.

'I suppose we could trespass. Get a better view,' he said out loud, looking around to see if there was any kind of entrance through the barbed wire.

'I'm not sure we should,' said

Gemma. 'I can't understand why it's been neglected so long. The last owner used to keep it in good order. Quite fond of it he was. Used to come up here and read in the summer months when I was a girl, or bring a chair and his binoculars and do some bird watching — kept a notebook of all the different birds he could recognise.'

'Looks like the new owner isn't as loving,' observed Dan, pulling a little at the barbed wire. 'Can't find an entrance.'

'Oi you, this is private property,' a voice shouted from the trees.

Dan and Gemma turned towards the voice and saw two men approaching. One was in his fifties with a goatee beard. He was dressed for the part, a country tweed suit, a walking stick in his hand. The other was younger with sandy hair, dressed in jeans and jacket.

'Can't you read the sign?' said the older of the two. 'It's not safe.'

'Sorry,' said Dan. 'My friend is from

these parts and was telling me about the folly. She used to come here as a child. I was intrigued and asked her to show me where it was.'

'Yes,' said Gemma, following Dan's lead. 'I have so many happy memories of playing here. I'm Gemma Lewis, by the way. This is my friend Dan Jackson.' She turned towards the building. 'Such a shame.'

'Hugo Tovey,' said the older man reaching out and shaking their hands. 'This is my estate manager, Ian Norton. Sorry, but I'm afraid it's far too dangerous for anyone to enter.'

'Doesn't look too bad to me,' observed Dan, looking once more at the structure.

'Looks can be deceiving,' said Tovey, waving away Dan's comment. 'I've had a team of surveyors going over the place. It's crumbling away inside. A piece of masonry could land on your head without warning. I'm going to get it fixed at some point but at the moment there is too much work to be done on the main house to worry about this building.'

'Pity,' said Dan. 'I was thinking of adding it to my next travel brochure. It would be something of interest to my readers.'

Gemma stared at Dan. He hadn't mentioned anything to her about a new travel brochure. She opened her mouth to say something but a quick look from Dan and she kept quiet.

'I'm a travel writer,' he said to the older man. 'Freelance. Sell my stuff to international magazines that are looking for places of interest such as this.'

'Well, I'm sorry but I'm afraid that you'll have to miss out on this one. As I've said it needs quite a bit of work doing to it and at the moment my priorities lie elsewhere. The last owner allowed all and sundry to visit the place and I'm afraid his upkeep of the building was not up to much. It's just not safe for anyone to enter.'

Gemma opened her mouth to say something. It was a lie. Colonel Withers was always spending money on the folly's upkeep. Every year, just before the summer season began, there would be workmen doing the necessary repairs. She caught a look in Dan's eye and his brief shake of the head. For some reason he wanted her to keep quiet.

'Pity,' said Dan. 'When Gemma first mentioned this place, I thought it would be great. I mean, there must quite a bit of history here. Isolated like it is and overlooking the bay. Almost as if it's watching for something to happen out there.' Dan nodded towards the sea.

'If you leave me your card I'll let you know when it's a better time to look around, although I'm not sure how long that will be. A couple years, I should think,' replied Tovey, stroking his beard.

Silence hung in the air.

'You'll be on your way, then,' said Tovey, not moving from his spot. 'Sorry I couldn't be of more help.'

'No worries,' said Dan, giving the man a smile. 'Plenty more sights to see before I decide what to send in. Sorry to have caused you so much trouble. Come on, Gemma, let's go.' He reached out and took Gemma's hand, gently pulling her towards the gate, not bothering to give Tovey his card. 'Didn't you say there were some old caves about five miles down the coast,' he raised his voice so that the two men could hear, 'and something to do with smugglers.'

They went through the gate and Dan took his time making sure it was secure while at the same time observing the men. Both were watching them, not moving from the spot. Dan raised his hand as a goodbye and guided Gemma towards the path.

'What was that all about?' she asked once they were out of view. 'I've never once mentioned caves and smugglers to you. And another thing, that Tovey man was lying about the Colonel — he kept the folly in good repair.'

'I believe you,' said Dan. 'There's something not quite right about them.

I can't quite put my finger on it but I'm sure they were watching us before they came out from behind the trees.'

'Really?' Gemma looked puzzled.

'Yes, just as I was pushing against that barbed wire fence I could have sworn I saw something flash in the tree as though someone had a pair of binoculars and the sun had caught the glass. In fact, I'm positive that's what I saw.'

'You could be right. The younger one looked a bit suspicious to me. Is that why you mentioned the story about caves and smugglers to put them off the scent?'

Dan gave a grin. 'Best I could come up with on the spur of the moment,' he said. 'Diverting their attention seemed a good idea at the time. But we haven't finished with them yet. The folly has more to tell us, I'm certain of that.'

'I agree,' said Gemma. They needed to find out more about Hugo Tovey.

'So where to now?' asked Dan, as they walked back down the hill toward the bay.

Before Gemma could reply the ringing tone of Dan's mobile began. Pulling it from his pocket he stared at the screen before turning it off.

'Sorry about that. Nothing important. Now, where were we?'

Gemma felt slightly irritated but shrugged it off. 'The chemist shop where Penny worked. Check out Hayley, see if she knows anything. Also see Alan Bradshaw.'

'Alan Bradshaw. Who's he?'

'He's the owner.' Gemma shuddered. 'Gives me the creeps.'

'How so?' asked Dan.

'Well, he sort of reminds me of a character out of the fifties. His hair is slick as though he's smothered it in hair cream and he wears some very untrendy shoes. Very pointy toes.'

'Pointy toes and slick hair,' remarked Dan, his lips twitching. 'Sounds like someone out of a B-rated movie.'

'You'll see what I mean when you meet him.'

'Can't wait,' replied Dan, his eyes twinkling with amusement.

Gemma looked back up the hill. 'What secrets does the folly hold, I wonder?'

'Well, I think there is something going on. Let's go to the chemist's first and then decide where to go from there.'

The double fronted shop was once a house. The word 'Bradshaw's' stood boldly written in black against a white background. A bell rang out as Dan opened the door.

He looked around. It clearly wasn't a busy day. Apart from him and Gemma there was only a young shop assistant filling one of the shelves with boxes of tissues. He watched Gemma as she picked up some shower wash and approached the girl.

'Hi, Hayley.'

The girl looked up from her task. 'Oh, hi Gemma. How are you?'

'Fine thanks Hayley. You?'

'Not too bad. So what can I do for you?' she said, moving towards the counter, but not before giving Dan a curious look. 'Although if you want a prescription, you'll have to come back. Mr Bradshaw's out at the moment and I'm not expecting him back for about half an hour. He's gone to pick up some supplies from the wholesalers.'

'No, just this,' said Gemma, placing the wash on the counter. 'Hope you're not missing Penny since she left. I spoke to her a couple of weeks ago. She's enjoying her new job.'

She hoped she sounded casual enough not to arouse any suspicion but from what she remembered, Hayley loved to gossip.

'Is she? That's good. To be honest I haven't heard from her since she left the bay, but there again, why should I? It's not as though we were best buddies.'

'Oh, I thought you got quite friendly after I moved. Always going out together, or so I heard.'

Hayley giggled. 'Oh that,' she said and then frowned as though she was considering what to say next. She must have come to the conclusion that it was OK. 'Her dad didn't approve of her new fella. She didn't want to hurt her dad's feeling so asked me to cover for her when they met up. No skin off my nose, so I said it was fine with me. As I said, not seen or heard from her since she left.'

'Well, thanks for clearing that up,' said Gemma, relief that little mystery was solved.

'Her bloke comes in, though,' said Hayley.

Of course he would, thought Gemma. Just because Penny moved to London it wouldn't stop Brian doing his job as a rep. Stupid of her not to think of that. She saw Dan's eyebrows rise slightly at the mention of Brian before he moved away to study items on one of the shelves.

'Never get a chance to speak to him,'

said Hayley. 'He comes in about once a month but Mr Bradshaw usually deals with him. He's always gone when I get back'

'Get back? What do you mean, get back?'

'Well, I always seem to be going out on an errand when he turns up. You know, Mr Bradshaw wants his suit from the cleaners or could I pick up his meat order from the butchers. I usually only have time to say hello before he's left the shop. Odd that, isn't it — '

Hayley popped the shower wash in a bag and Gemma handed over her money.

Hayley frowned. 'Although he was here a couple of weeks ago when I got back from the bakery. Mr Bradshaw said he fancied a cream cake with his elevenses. Always likes his cake, does Mr Bradshaw.'

Gemma watched Dan study a shelf full of aftershave, hoping Hayley would get to the point.

'Got him a nice chocolate eclair. His

favourite. Anyway Brian was here when I got back. I asked him if he wanted a cup of coffee but he said he was just leaving.'

The doorbell rang, announcing another customer, and Gemma had no more time to ask questions.

'Well, I'll leave you to your customers. Take care, Hayley.'

'Bye,' said Hayley before turning her attention back to the young mother with a toddler who began screaming as soon as they reached the shop counter.

'So, what do you think?' asked Gemma as they stepped outside onto the street.

'Not sure,' said Dan, scratching his chin. 'There's nothing you could call odd about anything Hayley has told us.'

'So you think our visit was a waste of time?'

'I wouldn't say that.' He shrugged. 'All information is useful, but I'd like to meet up with Mr Bradshaw.'

They began walking towards the

seafront, saying nothing, lost in their own thoughts.

'How do you fancy a midnight walk, Gemma?' asked Dan after a few minutes of silence.

At first she thought he meant a romantic walk and immediately wished she didn't have such conflicting emotions about the man by her side. She glanced at him and saw the frown on his face, realising his intentions were completely different.

'Go on,' she encouraged, wondering what he had in mind.

'The folly. I think we should take a look inside. What do you think?'

Gemma shivered, unsure if it was from fear of being caught or the excitement of it all. She smiled, forgetting Penny for a moment before sobering at the reminder of her missing friend.

'OK, I'm up for it.'

'Great.' Dan checked his watch. 'Look, I'm going off to buy a couple of torches. I'll meet you at the bottom of the harbour walk at eight o'clock. It will be dark by then. Hopefully we'll find out once and for all if the folly is just as dangerous as Tovey makes out or if there is something more sinister going on.'

'OK, I'll see you later,' said Gemma, wishing they could go now but realising it was too dangerous to try and gain access again during daylight hours.

She watched as Dan headed towards a bank of shops, one selling hardware. He reached into his pocket and pulled out his mobile. What was it about that man and his phone?

4

As it turned out the trip to investigate the folly was abandoned. A swell from the east turned a calm sea into a storm that tossed waves against the rocky headland making it dangerous to walk along the cliffs.

Gemma rang Dan to apologise. 'I've seen these storms before. The sea is vicious and should be respected.'

'OK. Disappointing, but I will go with your expert advice.'

'My mother wants to know if you'd like to come for supper?' she said, changing the subject. 'Well, that's if you want to,' she continued when he didn't reply.

He seemed to come out of whatever thinking zone he was in. 'Sorry. Of course, I'd love to come for supper.'

'Wonderful, I'll borrow Dad's car. It's too far for you to walk in this weather.

I'll pick you up about seven o'clock. Is that OK?'

'Perfect. See you then.'

Gemma put the phone down and headed to her mother's small work room at the back of her parents' bungalow.

Carol Lewis sat at her work bench, her head bent down in concentration and she rubbed away at the stone folded in between her polishing cloth.

'Dan accepted your invitation,' said Gemma, peering over her mother's shoulder. 'Can I look?'

'I found it on the shore this morning,' Carol said, holding up the dark blue stone, a thin grey vein curling around the middle. 'It'll look great in a silver setting hanging from a chain.'

Gemma agreed. Her mother's talent for spotting unusual stones and shells that washed up on the shore and turning them into jewellery was a wonder to her although why that should be when she'd passed her artistic genes onto her daughter she couldn't imagine.

Carol turned her head and looked over her bifocals at her daughter. 'Are you going to tell me what's going on?'

'Going on?' Gemma stalled, avoided her mother's eyes.

'Well, let's see. You phone up out the blue and say you're coming home for the weekend. You arrive and dash out again. Disappear first thing this morning. Then you mention someone called Dan who you want me to invite for supper. Are you surprised that I wonder what's going on?'

Gemma sat down on the easy chair in the corner of the room and sighed. She'd been shying away from this conversation since arriving home. 'I'm not sure where to begin.'

'The beginning would help,' said her mother, turning to face her daughter.

'It's Penny.'

'Penny Tremayne? What about her?'

Gemma let the story unfold while her mother sat still, listening to every word she said without making a comment.

'So that's why I'm here and why Dan came with me.' She sighed and bit down on her lip.

'Are you absolutely sure they're missing? Not gone off on a mini break and forgot to tell you?'

'We're talking about Penny here, Mum. You know how precise she is about arrangements.'

'True, but I still don't think it's a good idea that you go chasing after clues that could be just a load of nonsense.'

Gemma bristled at the accusation. 'It's not nonsense, Mum. I just know something is wrong. What about the folly?'

'True,' said Carol, turning back to her work bench and picking up the stone she was polishing before returning to face her daughter. 'The pair of you loved to go up there when you were kids until that episode when you nearly fell over the cliff top. Never went up there again. Can still see the terrified look on your face when your father mentioned we might go for a picnic up there not long after.'

'Well, I must have come a long way since then. I managed to walk up there yesterday with Dan.'

'Good for you but I'm still not happy about you doing detective work on your own. That's your trouble. You're too impulsive.'

Gemma bristled under the criticism. But before she could comment her mother continued.

'Look at what happened with Robbie. Only knew him five minutes and you up and left your home and went off to London.'

'Thanks for reminding me, Mum. As if I could forget.' She bent her head, not wanting to look at her mother and see the disappointment she knew she would see in her eyes.

Carol's voice gentled. 'Hey, I'm sorry I shouldn't have mentioned him. I just want you to look at the bigger picture and don't rush into anything.'

'I'll be fine, Mum. Penny's in some kind of trouble, I'm certain and I'm going to find her, with or without the help of the police or anyone else. Anyway Dan's of the same mind. He's certain that something is wrong. He'll keep me safe.'

'You like him, don't you? Do I detect romance in the air?'

Gemma burst out laughing, mostly to hide the fact of her growing attraction to Dan. Her mother wanted nothing more than to see her daughter walk up the aisle, although Gemma couldn't see the possibility of that happening for a long time. She was more than happy to stay single and work on her career.

'Mum, we've only known each other for a couple of days. OK, he's nice and I like him. Don't go picking out a wedding outfit just yet because it's not going to happen.'

Carol held up her hands. 'OK. You're just friends. I believe you.'

Gemma shook her head, noting a twinkle in her mother's eye. She stood up. 'You finish up here and I'll go and prepare the vegetables for supper.'

'Thanks, love,' said Carol, returning to face her work bench, 'Won't be long.'

As Gemma closed the door she heard her mother mutter. 'Heavens knows what her father's going to say about this.'

★ ★ ★

Dan huddled down into his jacket as he waited outside The Ship. Waves were crashing against the sea defences spraying the road and shop fronts with a salty wash. Strong winds whipped his hair across his face and he bent his head against the storm. A car pulled up and he looked up to see Gemma in the driver's seat, waving her hand to get his attention.

'The elements are certainly angry tonight,' he said, swiping his fingers through his hair and scrubbing salt water off his face as he buckled himself in. 'Do you ever get used to it?'

69

Gemma pushed the vehicle into gear, the wind buffeting against the car as they travelled along the pier.

'A storm is just part and parcel of living on the coast. Treat it with respect and you're OK.'

Dan nodded, agreeing with her statement. 'I've bought a bottle of wine. Hope that's OK?' He held up a bottle that Gemma hadn't noticed.

'My mum will love you,' said Gemma, a grin forming on her lips.

'Ah, a wine drinker.'

'She's been known to have one or two glasses in the evening.'

Dan chuckled. 'So tell me a bit about your parents, Gemma.'

'Bob and Carol Lewis. They run the gift shop on the seafront. Dad runs the shop and Mum makes jewellery and trinkets out of all sorts of stuff that the sea throws up.'

'Sounds like an idyllic life.'

Gemma thought for a moment. Idyllic sounded about right. 'Good word. Although I'm not sure my parents would agree when they are tired after a long day of summer tourists looking for gifts,' she said. 'I used to help out in the shop until I moved to London. Thought I'd do it forever but things didn't work out that way.'

Dan picked up on the sudden wistfulness in her voice. 'Regrets?'

Gemma shook her head. 'No, I don't think so, although maybe I should have thought it out a little better at the time.'

Dan noticed her biting down on her lip again and he was about to ask her what she meant when the car pulled into a driveway in front of a white bricked bungalow.

'Here we are,' said Gemma unbuckling her seat belt. She opened her door. 'Ready to make a run for it.' The wind whipped away her words and she ran toward the porch, Dan following right behind her.

Carol must have been on the lookout for them and the door opened immediately. 'Come in, come in,' she said waving Dan into the hallway. 'Goodness, what a night.'

'Good to meet you Mrs Lewis,' said Dan, reaching out to shake her hand.

'It's Carol,' she said, placing her hand in his. 'Come on through and meet my husband.'

Dan settled himself on the cream leather settee while Penny and her mum busied themselves laying the table and running back and forth into the kitchen. He missed family life, remembering when his parents were alive and meal times were full of laughter. He missed talking to his father about his accomplishments at school and how they'd go out on family outings. His mother's soft voice as she read him bedtime stories and smoothed his hair away from his face as sleep overtook him. His grandmother had done her best but it wasn't the same.

Dan took the glass of wine Bob offered him

'So my daughter tells me you're a travel writer.'

'That's right, Bob,' replied Dan, 'Just returned from China.'

'Tell me more.'

Dan began to relax as he related tales of the numerous countries he'd visited. He could see by the look on Bob's face that he wasn't just being polite, he was showing a genuine interest.

'OK, supper is served,' announced Carol, as she placed a large dish of root vegetables on the table. Gemma followed carrying a large dish of golden brown lasagne. Dan's taste buds went into overdrive trying to remember when he'd last tasted a home cooked meal. Takeaways or hotel food just wasn't the same.

The meal was delicious. Together with the wine there was a lot of laughter and telling of tales from both sides of the table. Bob told humorous stories of holidaymakers who visited the shop and Dan told them tales of people he'd met on his travels but hanging in the room all the time was the subject of Brian and Penny which nobody was mentioning.

A couple of times he looked over at Gemma and saw a frown or two and the worrying nibble on her lip. He wondered what it would be like to kiss away her troubles, then frowned himself. She was getting under his skin and he wasn't sure he liked it one bit. Friendship was fine, anything else was off limits. He didn't have time for a relationship in his life. He was too much of a restless soul. A home base was fine but travelling was what he loved best and what woman in her right mind would want that? Most girls he met wanted to settle down and have a family. He just didn't see that life in his future.

It was only when the meal was finished and the table cleared that the disappearance of Brian and Penny was brought up.

Cup of coffee in hand, Bob look straight at Dan. 'So we've been avoiding it all evening but I think now is the time to tell us about this goose chase you and my daughter are involved in.'

'Dad,' protested Gemma, before Dan could say anything.

'It's OK, Gemma,' said Dan, raising a hand, 'your father has every right to ask the question. I'd do exactly the same if I was him.'

Dan cradled his coffee cup and looked directly at Bob. 'I'm not convinced it is a wild goose chase. If I didn't think that my brother and Penny were missing I wouldn't have agreed to follow Gemma here.'

'So you don't think leaving it to the police is the best idea?' said Bob. He leant forward, cupping his chin in between his hands.

'They're looking in one direction. We're just going in another.'

'A dangerous other?'

Dan shrugged. 'If I hadn't agreed to come with Gemma she would have only looked into the folly on her own.'

'Well, I must admit my daughter is one of those who *does* before she thinks.'

'Oh, charming,' said Gemma. 'Just talk about me as though I'm not in the room.' She leant back in her chair with a big sigh making both men laugh out loud.

'OK. But be careful, my daughter is rather precious to me and her mother. Promise me if you get any kind of lead you'll go straight to the police and let them handle it.'

Dan nodded in agreement.

'Dad,' said Gemma, moving the conversation on, 'do you know what's going on at the folly? We went up there but it's all fenced off. We met the new owner. He told us it was dangerous and that's why he'd put a barrier in place and a warning sign.'

'So you've met Hugo Tovey.' There was a note of disgust in his voice.

'I gather you don't like him,' said Gemma.

Carol sighed. 'I think I'll make another cup of coffee. Once your father starts talking about our new local landowner, we could be here all night.'

'I'm not sure I'm that bad,' said Bob, passing his cup over to his wife for a refill.

'So, what's the story behind Tovey?' asked Dan, leaning forward in his chair, intent on hearing whatever Bob was going to say.

'Well, it's not so much what he's done as what he hasn't. I'm on the local council so anything that goes on around Westlea Bay, I usually know about. He arrived in the Bay just after you left for London,' said Bob, looking at his daughter. 'Anyway he arrives at a council meeting not long after he purchased the Manor, all guns blazing. Making promises about how he was going to upgrade the house. He plans to turn it into a conference centre. Promises to bring lots of business into the town. Jobs for local people during the winter months when things are quiet.'

'Surely that's a good thing?' said Dan

'It is,' agreed Bob. 'If he'd done what he'd promised . . . '

'He's done nothing,' said Carol, handing out fresh cups of coffee.

'Nothing at all?' said Bob, waving a hand about in disgust. 'He received planning permission about six months ago but since then nothing has been done. Every time the council ask him when the building work will start he comes up with an excuse, the latest being that the craftsmen he wants to carry out specialist work aren't available at the moment. It's all rot, of course. There's a lot of building work that can go ahead without specialised workmen. The hall needs updating now before it falls down. Colonel Withers, the previous owner, let the place go as he got older.'

'Was the folly neglected as well,' said Gemma.

Bob shook his head. 'Not sure about that. You know how much the Colonel loved that place. He always kept it in good repair.'

Gemma nodded in agreement.

Bob scrubbed a hand across his chin.

'You know, it's strange but as soon as he bought Westlea Manor he fenced off the folly. Hadn't thought much about that, but it's odd, don't you think?'

'Perhaps once Tovey checked it out it was in a worst condition than was first thought,' said Dan, trying to find a reasonable explanation.

Bob shook off the idea. 'No, I don't think so. I must confess I don't like the man. There's something not quite honest about him. I only wish I could put my finger on what it is. Did you meet his henchman?'

Gemma burst out laughing. 'Henchman. Oh really, Dad. Isn't that going a bit too far?'

'Ian Norton, that's his name. Calls himself an estate manager. If he's an estate manager I'm a rocket scientist.'

'What gives you the idea that he isn't?' enquired Dan.

'Simple. His hands. Never seen a day's hard work in their life. Too soft by far. Noticed them when he came to a council meeting with Tovey. He's another chap I don't trust.'

'But what would they have to do with Brian and Penny?' asked Carol. 'I can't imagine them mixing in the same company.'

'Neither can I,' agreed Dan.

'Well, we'll just have to find out if there's a connection,' said Gemma, 'because the more I think about it, something is going on and Brian and Penny have got themselves involved in it.'

'Told you she was headstrong,' said Bob giving his daughter a smile. 'Look, just be careful and if you find out anything contact the police. That's all I ask.'

'I promise, Dad.' Gemma rose from her seat, settled herself on the arm of her father's chair and gave him a hug.

Dan checked his watch and stood up. 'Time I headed back to the hotel. Can I phone for a taxi?'

'Nonsense,' said Gemma, 'I'll take you, Dan.'

'Not sure I want you driving me

home in this storm. It's been getting worse all evening.'

'I'll be fine driving, but thanks for being so chivalrous.'

'You make me sound like a knight in shining armour,' he said, his eyes sparkling with laughter.

'Come on, let's get our coats before I change my mind,' she said hastily, dismissing any thoughts of Dan dressed in shining armour riding a white horse.

She was just about to open the front door when Dan's mobile rang. She watched him pull it out of his pocket and frown when he saw who was on the caller display.

'Who is it?' she asked.

'The police,' he mouthed as he took the call.

Gemma felt a quiver of fear run through her. She hoped it was good news but by the look on Dan's face her hopes were diminishing fast.

'OK, fine,' said Dan. 'See you then. Bye.'

Gemma watched him pocket his

mobile, the frown still on his face.

'Well?' she asked when he said nothing.

'Nothing new.' He shrugged on his jacket. 'They haven't found Brian's car, or them for that matter. As they've now been missing for forty-eight hours or more they are going to up the search. They want to look around the flat. See if there are any clues.'

'But we did that already. There was nothing to find there.'

'I know, but its procedure.' Dan sighed. 'Anyway, I need to get back to London tomorrow and let them in. Stupid me, I should have thought to leave them a key before we left.'

'They should be looking down here for them in Westlea Bay. I hope you tell them that when you meet up with them tomorrow.'

'We haven't really got anything to tell them, though. Have we?'

Gemma felt like stamping her feet in frustration but refrained from doing so as she suddenly noticed her parents were standing in the hallway watching her exchange with Dan.

'I suppose not,' she agreed, albeit reluctantly.

Dan thanked Bob and Carol for their hospitality and followed Gemma out to the car. Little was said by either of them. Dan deep in thought, Gemma concentrating on the road as she controlled the car against the raging storm.

'I'll text you when I get back here, tomorrow,' he said as the car stopped outside The Ship.

'Oh, you're coming back then?' asked Gemma, her hands gripping the steering wheel.

Dan looked surprised. 'Of course.'

'I just thought that now the police were investigating, you wouldn't need to . . . '

Dan reach out and took one of her hands off the steering wheel and engulfed it in his own. 'My brother and his girlfriend are missing. There is no way I wouldn't stop searching for them.

With or without the help of the police. Anyway, we're a team, aren't we?'

His voice was gentle as he spoke and he slowly rubbed his thumb along he palm of her hand. Gemma's grip relaxed. She couldn't understand the relief she felt at his words but for the moment she was just happy that he was coming back.

She turned and gave him a smile, 'Yes, we're a team. Text me your arrival, I'll pick you up from the station.'

He reached out and gave her a kiss on the cheek. 'See you tomorrow,' he whispered before opening the car door and heading into the pub.

Gemma touched her cheek. She was in trouble. She just hoped Dan wasn't another Robbie.

5

Dan stood watching the car disappear from view. Gemma was getting under his usual calm exterior. He knew she was holding something back. He'd noticed a faraway look cross her face occasionally. He'd wondered what she was thinking about. He wanted to dig deeper. He shook his head, trying to rid his brain of random thoughts. Deciding against going straight to his room he headed towards the hotel bar hoping a drink would soothe his chaotic thoughts.

The bar wasn't busy. A couple of men sat at a table near the fire playing dominoes. A man in his twenties was sipping a pint and reading a book. The only other people were three men huddled in the corner talking quietly between themselves.

He caught sight of Whitey sitting at

the bar nursing a drink. He raised a hand in acknowledgement and walked over to her.

'Quite a night out there,' he said, shrugging off his jacket.

'It sure is, dearie,' said Whitey picking up her glass and raising it to her lips. 'You look as though you could do with a drink.' She nodded to the barman. 'On me,' she said with a smile.

'Thanks. A pint of bitter.'

He looked around the room before sitting on the only other bar stool available. 'I'm surprised to see you have any customers. Hotel guests?'

'No, not all. Reg and Bill, over there, are regulars.' Whitey chuckled. 'Never miss a night playing dominoes, even in the worst of weather.'

'Brave men,' observed Dan, picking up his pint of bitter.

'Weather beaten fishermen, used to the storms. Nothing will stop them coming out of an evening.' She smiled.

'I admire them,' said Dan, swallowing

a mouthful of beer and appreciating the taste.

'Mr Ellard, over there reading the book, is staying the night. He's got a job interview in the morning, so he tells me.'

Whitey took another sip of her drink. 'The other two over in the corner talking to Alan are sailors. Their ship is anchored out to sea and has broken down. They're waiting for a part for something or other. According to them it was supposed to be ready but there's a delay. They intended to head back to their ship but the storm blew in so they are staying the night.'

'And Alan?' asked Dan.

'My, you're a nosy one,' said Whitey, raising an eyebrow.

'Sorry,' said Dan, giving a wry smile. 'Put it down to my natural interest in people.'

'Natural interest?'

'I'm a writer.'

'A reporter?'

'Oh no, not at all,' he reassured. 'I'm

a travel writer. That's why I'm here. Checking out places of interest for an article.'

Dan took a sip of his beer wondering why he'd said that. Gemma told him it wasn't a good idea for everyone to know what they were doing so it sounded plausible. He better remember to tell Gemma just so they got their story straight.

'Places of interest?' asked Whitey. 'Wouldn't have thought Westlea Bay was that interesting in the winter.'

Dan thought quickly, 'Oh, I'm not writing about towns. Its buildings I'm interested in. Gemma told me about the folly up on the cliffs and it gave me an idea for an article. People like to visit stuff that's unusual so I thought I'd check it out. Hence why I'm here.'

Dan drained the last of his beer feeling quite pleased with the tale of checking out buildings of interest. It was a great idea and would stop anyone asking questions about him and Gemma nosing around.

'So, have you visited the folly yet?'

'Another drink?' he asked Whitey, pushing his glass towards the barman who seemed to do nothing but wipe the counter and clean glasses.

'Gin and tonic would be good,' said Whitey, tapping the rim of her glass with her finger.

'Gemma and I went to see the folly but it looks as though I'm out of luck. It's all fenced off and has danger notices posted. We did meet the owner though. He explained that it was unstable and need repairs before he could let us have a look round.'

'Oh, so you've met our new land-owner? What do you think of him?' She shifted in her seat causing a rope of bells hanging around her neck to ring softly.

'Seemed reasonable enough. Shame that he wouldn't let me take a look at the folly though. Even if it needs repairs I could have taken a couple of pictures and seen the damage myself. It would have been an added attraction to my article. Explaining to the readers what can happen when historical buildings are left in disrepair.'

'If? You said 'if' the folly needs repairs. Are you doubting what he said to you?'

Dan shook his head. 'Not at all. Just a figure of speech. I'm sure he's quite correct. By the way, what do you think of him yourself?'

Whitey shook her head. 'Not met him. Doubt he'd want to visit a place like this.' She looked around the bar and shrugged. 'Needs a lot money spending on it.'

Dan looked at her, surprised at the sudden change of subject.

'It's not that bad,' said Dan, glancing around and taking in the dated wallpaper and furnishings. 'It has character.'

Whitey burst out laughing.

'Oh, it has that all right.'

'So as I'm such a nosy person, care to tell me what brought you to Westlea Bay, Whitey. You're not a local.'

'How did you guess?' she asked.

Dan grinned. 'Your accent. If I'm right I detect a touch of London in you.'

Whitey nodded. 'Very clever. Yes, you're right. I lived there for the first fifteen years of my life.'

'You know Whitey, I have a feeling you're a lady who has a few tales to tell.'

Whitey fiddled with her bangles. 'Not much to tell really. I grew up in the sixties. A time of great social change. What's the saying, 'If you remember the sixties, you weren't really there?''

'I seem to remember that quote from somewhere.' He smiled.

Whitey looked away into the distance as if remembering a time long gone, before returning her gaze to Dan. 'It's not true, of course. I remember it as though it was yesterday. The summer of love, music festivals, flowers in your hair . . . '

'Sounds as though you had a ball,' said Dan, a smile playing on his lips at the thought of Whitey and all that free love.

'Oh, I did indeed, dearie,' she said matching his grin.

'So how come you ended up here in the bay? I wouldn't have thought it was at the heart of all that loving.'

Whitey waved a hand. 'Well you're wrong there. In fact, it was all to do with Westlea Manor.'

He raised an eyebrow. 'Really?'

Whitey straightened her long flowing skirt and rested her hand on her lap. 'I was a bit of a wild child in my youth,' she said. She gave a little chuckle and shrugged. 'I know I don't look it now, being a respectable landlady of an establishment, but in those days it was so different. I grew up in a small village where nothing ever happened.'

Dan nodded but said nothing, letting her continue with her tale.

'I was a teenager in the sixties and everything was so refreshing. I wanted to try everything. Go where the most popular crowd went. So I followed. To put in simply, I left Limpsfield for wider pastures.'

'Didn't your parents object?'

She shook her head and a coldness came into her eyes. 'That's a tale for another time.'

'OK,' said Dan. It was obviously a subject that she was not happy to delve into.

She continued. 'So I followed the flow. Did the parties. Did the music concerts along the coast until I ended up here. Some guy, a lower member of the aristocracy bought Westlea Manor and wanted to turn it into one of those self-sufficiency places that were beginning to become popular. You know the sort, grow everything yourself, keep a few cows and goats, chickens, and a few other animals. He wanted to create his only little haven for like-minded people.'

'It didn't work?'

'Oh, yes, it did for a while and it was wonderful even though I say it myself. It was all peace and love and nobody to tell you what to do.'

'So what changed?'

'People did. Some grew up and moved on. Wanted what their parents had. You know, the house and the children — respectability.' She picked up her glass and took a sip before carrying on with her tale.

'Anyway, the aristocrat was persuaded to re-join the masses after pressure from his family. Money being cut off or something like that. I can't remember now. So he sold up and we had to move on.'

'So how come you stayed?'

'A man. What else.' She winked and shifted on her stool. 'Rod Whitely. His parents owned this place and they gave me a job after Westlea Manor. Rod and I became an item and I decided that respectability wouldn't hurt so I married him. There was a car crash . . . I lost Rod and his parents in one go.'

Dan saw the pain in her eyes and kept quiet. There was nothing he could say.

Whitey gave a heavy sigh. 'So that's my life story. Care to share yours?'

Dan drained the last of his pint and stood up. 'I think I'll leave that for another day. It's getting late. I think I'll turn in.'

Whitey looked at the old grand-mother clock hanging on the wall and nodded. 'Before you go, I wondered how long are you planned on staying?'

'Not sure,' said Dan, picking up his jacket. 'Is it a problem? The room is still available for a while, isn't it?'

'Oh yes. As I said when you booked in, it's quiet this time of year. I just like to be aware of how long my guests plan on staying, that's all.'

'OK. Well I'll let you know in good time when I'm leaving. Goodnight Whitey.'

'Night, dearie.' She finished off her gin and tonic and nodded to the barman for a refill.

★   ★   ★

Dan shrugged off his jacket and put his wallet on the dresser before reaching for his laptop and checking for the train times. He rubbed tired eyes. His jet lag was still lingering and he hoped that another good night's sleep would get his body clock back on track.

Thoughts of Gemma crept into his mind. He hoped she got home safely. Maybe he should ring her, just to check. He reached for his phone and dialled her number before he changed his mind.

After a couple of rings she picked up. 'Hi Dan. Is something wrong?'

He could hear the worry in her voice and cursed at himself for ringing so late.

'No, all's fine,' he quickly assured her. 'I was just checking that you got home all right. I should have rung earlier.'

'So why didn't you?'

He heard a rustle and wondered what she was doing. Probably getting comfortable in bed.

'I got chatting to Whitey in the bar. I'm sorry it's so late. I didn't wake you, did I?'

'I was sketching. It helps me relax and I get my best ideas late at night.'

'What are you drawing?' he asked. They never discussed in detail Gemma's work although he'd seen for himself that she was gifted.

'The folly. When it was in its glory, not tied up with a bow of barbed wire like it is now.'

'I'd like to see it when it's finished. Talking about the folly, reminds me. I've told Whitey that's why I'm here.'

'You haven't told her about Brian and Penny? I thought we'd agreed.'

There was that alarm in her voice again.

'No, no. I've said nothing. I just told her that I was here to look around the area at different buildings of interest, mainly follies. Just like I mentioned to Tovey when we met him. Snooping around can be dangerous and it sounds like a good story for why I'm here.'

'I agree,' she said.

There was silence between the two of them and Dan decided it was time for him to say goodnight.

'I'll let you know when I'll be back tomorrow.'

'OK. I'll be at the station to pick you up. Let's hope you have some good news.'

'Yes, let's hope so. Goodnight Gemma,' he said softly.

'Goodnight, Dan.'

Dan waited until she disconnected first. He was thinking about her far too much. Brian was his first priority and he didn't have time for anything else in his life at the moment. He reached for his laptop bag and pulled out a notebook. He always thought better if he could see the facts in front of him.

He put his glasses on and began to write a list of all the leads he and Gemma has discovered so far. They didn't have too much to go on . . .

The folly

Fenced off

Hugo Tovey
Chemist Shop

He was sure there was a connection but he couldn't see it at the moment. As he settled into bed he only hoped that he had the time to put everything in place before it was too late.

6

Gemma woke the next morning from a restless night; a disturbing dream invading her sleep. Brian and Penny were stranded on a small boat out at sea. Gemma and Dan were swimming towards them but every time they were in reach a strong wave would sweep them away. In the end they gave up. The last she saw was Penny reaching out, arms wide and shouting for help.

She dragged herself out of bed and headed for the shower spending a long time under the hot spray to clear her head. She dressed and sat in front of the mirror combing her hair into a ponytail, securing it with an elastic band. Dark circles shadowed her eyes. Sleepless nights were not a good look.

Her thoughts turned to Dan. She was

surprised by his phone call the night before but was secretly pleased that he'd been thoughtful enough to check that she'd returned home safely. He was intruding more and more into her thoughts and Robbie the Rat was becoming a fading memory. She gave herself a little shake. Remembering the betrayal, she pushed thoughts of both men out of her head as she headed towards the kitchen.

A note by the kettle told her that both parents were out. Her mother would be on the beach if she wanted to meet up. Gemma wasn't surprised. Her mother loved nothing more than walking along the sandy carpet after a storm. Her basket under her arm, she'd collect all sorts of treasure to turn into something spectacular.

She gazed out of the window as she ate her breakfast. The storm from the night before had moved on, leaving a strong wind and grey sky. She packed her tote bag with her sketch pad and pencils. If she was lucky she might settle among the sand dunes, protected against the sea breeze and do some sketching. She shrugged on a warm jacket and headed along the coastal path towards the beach.

Grabbing the handrail to the steps leading down to the sand she looked along the stretch of beach in search of her mother. Spotting her in the distance, she watched as her mother squatted down, inspecting some form of treasure. Gemma smiled to herself. Her mother had the gift of finding a gem among the chaos, although she claimed that her biggest gem was found the day her daughter was born, hence naming her Gemma.

'Any good finds?' she asked as she approached her mother.

Carol lifted the basket at her side and ran her fingers over the shells and stones.

'There are a few. Take a look.' She held up the basket for Gemma's perusal.

Pearly shells and pebbles of all sizes

littered the bottom of the basket. Gemma could picture the little jewellery boxes that her mother would sell in the shop to the young girls looking for keepsakes to take home with them. The gift shop was a family affair. Bob made the boxes, coated them with varnish, then Carol would decorate them into works of art.

Gemma, up until her move to London, worked in the shop. She began designing cards as a side line to sell to visitors in the summer. It was one such visitor who had spotted her talent and urged her to try and sell her drawings to a wider audience. She'd managed to find a couple of companies who were interested in incorporating her drawings into their range. Her parents had been delighted that her talent was being appreciated and encouraged her to expand her business.

Looking at the find before her, Gemma reached out and picked up a flat pebble. Blue in colour, it reminded her of Dan's eyes. She dropped it quickly back to join the other collectables. Why does that man keep invading my thoughts? It was only three days ago she'd met him. Surely attraction didn't happen this quick? She should be concentrating on finding Penny.

'I was thinking of making it into a pendant,' said Carol. She took it from her daughter's hand and held it up to light. 'Unusual colour. Not seen one like it before.'

'Beautiful colour,' agreed Gemma watching her mother turn the stone over in her hand, even on a grey day like today, the shade was striking. Gemma could clearly see it set in silver, hung around some young girl's neck.

Carol got to her feet. 'Dan get off OK?'

Gemma shrugged. 'I suppose so, I've not heard from him this morning. He's going to text me his arrival time so I can meet him at the station.'

Carol nodded and began walking along the beach. 'I like him.'

Gemma eyed her mother and she fell into step alongside her. 'Don't go reading anything into our friendship when there's nothing there.'

'OK, OK. You've already warned me off. You're just friends.' Carol laughed, bending down to pick up a beautifully formed shell and holding up for inspection. 'Look at that. A Sunday Venus.'

Gemma peered at the shell, marvelling at her mother's knowledge.

'Once polished and bleached it will look exceptional as a bracelet. What do you think?'

Gemma studied the shell for moment before agreeing with her mother.

They began a slow walk along the shore, stopping occasionally as Carol found something of interest, either putting it into her basket or discarding it.

The wind began to pick up and Gemma shoved her hands in her pockets and huddled down into her jacket wishing she had been thoughtful enough to bring a scarf with her. She looked out to sea. The waves were building up a pace. White horses racing towards the finishing line.

'Looks as though the storm hasn't finished with us yet.'

Carol followed her gaze. 'Hmm. You're right.'

'I was going to settle down among the sand dunes and do some sketching but I think the wind will defeat me.'

'How's business?' asked Carol, shifting her laden basket from one arm to the other. 'You haven't mentioned it since you've been back.'

'Good. I've done a few commissions that have been well received and I'm considering expanding into online sales. You know, on the internet.'

Carol raised an eyebrow. 'I maybe be old but even I've heard of the internet.'

'Of course you have. Sorry. So what do you think?' Gemma always valued her mother's opinion and if she was going to branch out she would appreciate the nod of approval. 'Good idea?'

'Sounds like it. Have you done much research?'

'Well, a little. I'd need to get a website set up and then a considerable amount of web marketing but, you know me, never shy of hard work.'

'My daughter, ever the busy bee.'

Gemma laughed and nudged her mother on the shoulder. 'Now, I wonder who I take after?'

Carol joined in the laughter and linked her free arm into Gemma's. 'Come on, let's head home and have a warming cup of coffee.'

'You should think about marketing your jewellery online, Mum. Be a tidy income for you in the winter months.'

Carol didn't say anything for a moment and Gemma wondered if she had heard her or not. 'Mum, I said . . . '

'I heard you the first time,' said Carol as she kept walking, her head down and not looking at her daughter.

Not for the first time since Gemma had arrived home did she sense there was something on her mother's mind. A couple of times she thought her mother was going to say something before she seemed to change her mind.

'What's up, Mum?' she said, frowning. 'There's nothing wrong with you, is there?'

'No, I'm fine,' said Carol, 'and before you ask, so is your father.'

'Thank goodness for that,' said Gemma, sighing with relief. 'But there's something. Come on, tell me.'

'We've talked it over, your dad and I, and we've decided to sell the shop.'

Gemma looked at her mother, surprised at her announcement. 'Selling the shop? But why?'

Carol stopped walking and looked at her daughter. 'We've thought about it a lot over the last few months. You know how much your father wants to travel. We just decided to go farther afield than our own country.'

It was true, her father was always going on about travelling the world, following the ships that he saw out at sea every day. Gemma always thought it was just a pipe dream, she never thought her parents would actually consider it.

She didn't realise she'd said the words out loud until she heard her mother's voice.

'No pipe dream. We're actually going to do it. We just think it's the right time.'

Gemma nibbled on her lip. Her parents were a constant in her life. Always there to turn to. Apart from the odd holiday to Spain in the winter months, they'd never gone far.

'Are you selling the bungalow? How long will you be gone? How far are you going?' The questions came out in a rush of panic thinking she might not see her parents for a long time.

Carol began walking again.

'So many questions. OK, we won't be selling the bungalow, only the shop. And probably for a couple of years. Around the world. There you go. Does that answer all your questions?'

Gemma was still in shock and

couldn't get her tongue around the words she wanted to say so she just looked at her mother.

Carol continued her explanation. 'Look sweetheart. You're settled in London and am I right in thinking you have no intention of returning permanently home for good?'

Gemma nodded.

'No. I'm settled into my flat and like the city.'

'Good, that's what your father and I thought.'

Gemma had a sudden thought. 'You're not leaving just because I've moved?'

Carol shook her head. 'Not at all. Your dad and I are both pleased that you've done so well and that your art can give you a good living. As for the bungalow, we're going to rent it out for a couple of years, just for the income. We'd never leave here permanently, Westlea Bay will always be home.'

Gemma considered her mother's words. They were both hard working

110

people and deserved some time to themselves. She was being a little selfish wanting them to stay and always be there for her. No, her mother was right. It was their time and she was pleased for them.

She wrapped her arms around her mother and gave a crushing hug. 'I'm pleased for you. You and Dad will have such a great time. Promise me you won't worry about me while you're gone?'

'You're our daughter. We will always worry about you, that's what parents do,' said Carol, returning the hug. 'Come on, let's go and put the kettle on and I'll tell you all about our plans.'

7

Gemma was frustrated. After waiting all the previous day for Dan to ring, she finally received his call in the late afternoon. He'd decided the stay in London overnight. His article was finished and he wanted to visit his editor at his London office to discuss further projects. She could understand this. Getting the next commission was vital when you were freelance. When she asked him about the visit with the police he was noncommittal, just saying that he would tell her all about it when he got back the next morning. She wanted to question him further but he seemed a bit abrupt so she decided not to pursue the matter.

It was raining again. She covered her head with the hood of her jacket as she walked along the path. Would the bad weather ever ease? The red man at the pelican crossing outside the station halted her progress. She looked across the road. She could see Dan. He was talking to a blond-haired man, about his own age. They were deep in conversation. Had he brought a friend to help with the search? The red man turned green and she walked towards the pair, calling Dan's name as she approached. He looked up and waved and said something to his companion who gave her a quick glance before moving back towards the entrance of the station.

'A friend of yours?' she said.

'Who?' he asked, cupping her elbow and leading her back across the road.

'That man. The one you were talking too.'

'Oh, that man. Just someone asking for directions.'

'Did he get off at the wrong stop?'

'What? No, I don't think so? What makes you ask that?'

'Just that he headed back into the station.'

'I think he was going to pick up a map of the town. Anyway, he's just a stranger. Come on, let's get out of this rain and I'll tell you how I got on with the police.'

For some reason, Gemma wasn't quite sure that Dan was telling her the truth. They appeared too deep in conversation for just giving directions. Maybe she was over thinking it. Travellers got lost all the time in a seaside resort. Giving directions was something she'd often done herself. She pushed the doubts away, eager to find out about Dan's meeting with the police.

'There's a café on the seafront. It's one of the few that stays open this time of year. Come on, I'll treat you to a coffee and a piece of cake.'

'Fruit cake and you're on. Lead the way.'

The café was busy which was surprising. Holidaymakers — autumn tourists as Gemma thought of them. The hardy sort that preferred the colder months. There were some excellent walks along the coast and she noted a few backpacks were resting on the floor by their owners. Gemma looked around for a suitable table.

'Grab that table,' she said, indicating a spot by the window. 'I'll get the coffee.'

'So tell me. Is there any news?' she asked, a few minutes later as they both cut into large slabs of fruit cake.

'Well, not a lot I'm afraid. The police looked around. Couldn't find anything significant. Asked a few more questions. You know the sort. Was there any trouble in their relationship? Did they often go away at short notice? That sort of stuff.' He took a sip of coffee and shrugged. 'I'm afraid I wasn't much help, not really knowing them as a couple, although I could confirm that Brian is the least spontaneous person I knew. He always thinks things through. Well, he does now.'

Gemma was surprised by the comment.

'Does now?'

Dan sighed. 'Brian was a bit of a hellion in his youth. Would get into spots of bother. I think he was easily led. He was quite young when our parents died and he needed a father to guide him. I did my best but I was a poor second. He got caught shoplifting. It was the first time he'd ever attempted such a thing. The gang he hung about with had urged him on. Told him it was a test so that he could be part of their gang.' Dan popped a piece of cake into his mouth and stared out of the window.

'So, what happened?' asked Gemma after a minute of silence.

Dan looked back at Gemma and gave a wry smile. 'Brian wasn't much good at shoplifting. Thank goodness. Anyway the police put the fear of god into him. It did the trick. He changed friends. Began to work hard at school and vowed he would always think things through before he did anything stupid again.'

Gemma watched Dan take a drink from his cup. He seemed relieved that he'd told her. He was revealing more about himself and she liked what she saw. She reached out and touched his hand. 'I'm sure you did the best you could at bringing him up. You seem to blame yourself but remember you were only young yourself.'

'Maybe,' he admitted. 'But I was the elder. The one who knew better. I should have seen what was going on when he got mixed up with that gang.'

'What about your grandmother?'

'I'm not sure she really took much notice of us boys, apart from giving us the basics. She did her best but she was still reeling at the loss of her daughter. In fact, I don't think she ever got over it. Well you wouldn't, would you?'

'No, I suppose not,' said Gemma, not wanting to think about losing a child.

'Don't get me wrong, she loved us dearly, but I think she was at a loss on how to bring up two boys burgeoning on manhood.'

'I'm sure she did her best, as did you under the circumstances. I can't imagine what it would be like.' She shuddered at the thought of losing her parents, even the idea of their impending trip made her feel a loss.

'Anyway, what else did the police say?'

Dan looked relieved to move away from the subject of his parenting skills. 'Well they haven't found Brian's car as yet. They've checked his work and his office haven't heard from him although they didn't expect to as both he and Penny booked holiday time. Apparently they are not expecting them back for a couple of weeks. We looked for their passports but couldn't find them. The police are sure that's an indication that they've gone abroad for a couple of weeks. They've promised they'll keep on looking and will let me know if they find anything.'

Gemma gave a huff of frustration.

'Honestly, why would they have gone abroad if Penny invited me for the weekend? Are they really interested?'

'I'm sure they are,' Dan assured her. 'I suppose they're just cautious. Just in case it's a wild goose chase.'

Gemma leant back in her chair and traced an imaginary picture along the table top with her finger. 'So where do we go from here? Are they still going to look for them?'

'Of course,' said Dan, the surprise in his voice made Gemma look into those intense blue eyes of his. 'Nothing's changed. I still think you're right and Westlea Bay is the place where we should be looking. What the connection is, I don't know, but I'm sure we'll find out.'

'Did you tell the police about our own investigations?'

'Yes, but they advised me to leave it to them.'

'But you're not going too, are you?' she asked.

He shook his head. 'Not a chance.'

Gemma rolled her shoulders not realising how tense she's been and looked out the window. The heavy rain had eased into a light drizzle and the rivulets of water ran down the window. Something caught her eye and she frowned.

'Well, that's a surprise,' she murmured.

'What is?' asked Dan, following her gaze.

'Those two men. Over there.' She nodded towards the pier where two men stood talking.

Dan followed her gaze. 'That's Ian Norton, isn't it?'

Gemma nodded. 'Yes it is, but I'm surprised who he's talking to.'

'Oh?'

Gemma kept watching the two men. They seemed to be arguing. Ian Norton was gesturing with his hands, like he was trying to point out something to the other man.

'Gemma?' prompted Dan.

'That other man is Alan Bradshaw.'

'The owner of the chemist shop?' asked Dan. 'He was in The Ship last night.'

'Was he? Always thought his local was The Lobster Pot at the other end of the bay.'

'Perhaps he fancied a change?'

'Could be.'

The two men had finished their conversation and were walking away from the pier in different directions. 'I wonder what they have in common.'

Dan shrugged. 'Perhaps they're friends.'

'They didn't look very friendly. In fact, I would say they were having a row.'

'It certainly seemed that way,' agreed Dan.

Gemma thought for a moment. 'I think we need to know a bit more about Alan Bradshaw.'

'Surely you know quite a bit about him? Him being Penny's boss.'

Gemma pushed back her chair, buttoned up her coat and slipped her bag on her shoulder. 'That's just it. He was just her boss. We only ever had a nodding acquaintance with each other. Come on, we need to talk to my father.'

'Your father? Why?' Dan asked Gemma as she headed out of the café.

'Because he knows almost everyone in Westlea Bay,' she said, 'and I bet he knows a lot about Alan Bradshaw.'

8

Dan only walked a few steps before he realised Gemma was going in the wrong direction, with his long strides he quickly caught up with her.

'Err, where are we going?'

'I told you — to see my father. He's at the boat house.'

'Boat house?' Dan was none the wiser.

'He's doing repairs to his yacht,' explained Gemma as she hurried along the pier.

His yacht. What on earth was she talking about? Bob didn't look the sort to have loads of money. Well, not enough to buy a yacht, let alone maintain it. Unless, of course, the gift shop business was doing an absolute bomb in the summer months. He must have misheard her.

'You did say yacht?'

Gemma stopped walking and turned to him, smiling. 'I'll explain when we get there. Come on. It's at the end of the harbour.'

The boat house was a large wooden structure, with large double doors at the front. A sign hanging above the doors simply said 'BOB'S HOUSE'.

'Dad's little joke,' said Gemma, as Dan lifted an eyebrow. 'We'll go in the side door. Dad likes to keep the big doors shut. Keeps the salt from the sea from causing harm to the yacht.'

Dan was now completely confused. Surely a yacht would be used to sea water?

Gemma pushed open the door and stepped inside. 'Dad's yacht,' she said, sweeping her hand in front of her.

Dan followed her gaze and a smile slowly spread across his face. 'A yacht?' he said, chuckling as he looked at the large motorhome in front of him.

'A land yacht. That's what they're called,' explained Gemma, her eyes dancing with merriment. 'Sorry. I just couldn't help teasing you for a bit. Dad bought it a couple of years ago. It was in a bit of a sorry state and he's been working on it in his spare time ever since.'

'Did I hear my name mentioned?' said Bob, walking out from behind the large motorhome.

'You did,' said Gemma, walking over to her father and kissing him on the cheek. 'I was telling Dan about your hobby, although I might have stretched my imagination a bit.'

'Ah,' said Bob, wiping his hands with a cloth he pulled from his back pocket. 'She's been telling you I've got a yacht.' He tutted. 'Gemma, you really must stop doing that.'

Gemma laughed. 'Sorry, Dad. Just couldn't help it.'

Dan joined in the laughter. 'Well I was certainly fooled. Mind you, it does look an impressive machine.' He looked at the sleek lines of the motorhome, cream in colour with strips of two toned brown running along the sides.

Gemma groaned.

'Don't get him started. It's his pride and joy.'

'It certainly is,' said Bob. 'Come and have a look inside. Sleeps up to six, fitted air conditioning. The kitchen was a bit rough when I bought it but I'm almost got that put to rights.'

'Dad,' interrupted Gemma. 'Can you give Dan the guided tour another time? We need to talk to you about something else?'

'Nothing wrong, is there? You've not heard any bad news when you spoke to the police?' He turned his attention to Dan, a look of concern crossing his face.

'No, nothing like that,' said Gemma, interrupting again.

'So what got you all in a tiss?' asked Bob walking over to a table where an assortment of jars, bottles, tins and paint brushes lay cluttered on the top.

'I just wondered how much you knew about Alan Bradshaw?'

Bob looked at his daughter and

frowned. 'Alan Bradshaw. Why on earth do you want to know about him?'

'We've just seen him talking with Ian Norton, you know that estate manager chap from Westlea Manor. Just thought it was strange, that's all.'

Bob picked up a tin of varnish and examined the label. 'Wouldn't have thought those two were friends.' He shrugged. 'Possible, though.'

Bob prised the lid off the tin with a screwdriver and held it out to Gemma. 'What do you think for the shelving?'

Gemma took a peek inside. 'Bit too dark.'

Bob looked at it again and shrugged. 'Maybe you're right.'

'So, Dad. Alan Bradshaw?'

'Oh, yes, right,' said Bob, putting the lid back on the tin. 'Well as you know there's been a Bradshaw's in the town since I can remember. George Bradshaw was the chemist when I was a boy. Nice chap, always gave you a sweet if your mum picked up some horrible medicine for you to take when you were ill.'

Bob smiled at the memory before Gemma prompted him again.

'Ah, yes,' he continued. 'Well, George passed away about five years ago and Alan, his nephew, turned up to take over the business. Must admit all of us on the council were surprised. George had never married and as far as we were aware had no family, let alone, a nephew who happened to be a chemist. According to Alan, it was a profession that ran in the family with at least one of each generation taking up the occupation.' He took a deep breath before continuing. 'George left his nephew everything. The council thought the shop would be sold to one of those big companies but no, Alan wanted to keep it going. After much discussion the council decided that it would be a good idea to keep a family business in the community so after checking all his credentials he was given the go ahead to continue administering prescriptions to the public.' Bob picked up another tin of varnish and reached for his screwdriver. 'That's about all I know.'

Dan glanced across a Gemma as a look of disappointment crossed her face. It appeared that what Bob told her hadn't helped at all.

'So, you don't know anything else? Where he came from, maybe?'

'Oh, well he came from somewhere around London, that I do know. Think it was Croydon, but I can't be certain.' He looked up at his daughter, smiled and tapped his forehead. 'Your dad's brain cells don't work as hard as they used to — old age creeping up.'

Gemma snorted. 'You're as sharp as a button and you know it.'

'Maybe,' Bob admitted and went back to opening the tin in his hand. 'How about this one?' he asked holding it out to Gemma.

'Perfect,' she said, peering into the tin.

'So why do you think it's important that you saw Norton and Bradshaw together? I know Norton hasn't been here long but they could have become friends even in that short time.'

Gemma shoved her hands in her jacket pocket. 'Just seemed odd, that's all. They were arguing. A pretty strong argument by the look of it. Bradshaw was waving his hands in the air and Norton was getting red in the face.'

'So you're concluding that because they argued that there's some connection between that and Brian and Penny going missing?'

After listening to Bob's reasoning, even Dan had to admit it sounded a bit of a thin reason.

'Just a feeling I have, Dad,' said Gemma. She turned to Dan. 'What do you think?'

'Well, it's a possibility.' He was not sure he agreed with her but any lead was a good lead. At the moment there were only guesses and little information.

'Right,' said Bob, 'let's leave the detecting for a minute. Dan, come and have a look round my pride and joy.' He put down the tin of varnish and waved a hand towards the motorhome.

Dan look over to Gemma for confirmation. They could really do with checking out more about Bradshaw but he didn't want to be rude.

Gemma gave him a look of resignation and they both followed her father up the steps and into the home.

Dan had to admit he was impressed. Most of the work looked completed. A rich blue carpet was fitted in the main living area. Seating covered in a dove grey complimented the soft cream of the walls. High level cupboards were fitted along both sides. A closed door was at the far end. On further investigation this opened up into a bedroom. The furnishings were of high quality. A varnished wooden floor finished off the effect of a job well done. Another door led to a bathroom. Dan had to admit, Bob's DIY abilities were excellent.

'Impressive. Looks good to go,' said

Dan, running his hands along the moulding at the edge of the door frame.

'Just the kitchen to finish,' said Bob, turning back towards the living area.

'Gosh, Dad, you've excelled yourself this time. I almost wish I was going with you,' said Gemma, taking in all her father's hard work.

Bob looked at his daughter. 'You're OK with our plans?'

Dan looked at Gemma and then her father. Had he missed something? Where were Bob and Carol going?

'Well, I was a bit shocked at first,' said Gemma, sitting down on one of the plush benches, 'but I think it's a great idea.' She turned to Dan and explained about her parents plans.

'Sounds like a trip of a lifetime, Bob,' said Dan, shoving his hands in his pockets and rocking back on his heels. 'Let me know which countries you plan to visit. I might know a few places of interest to view.' He sighed. 'Almost makes me wish I was going with you.'

'But you travel all the time,' said Gemma.

Dan chuckled. 'True, but it's always work. Different if I was on holiday and could relax but I'm always on a deadline.'

'I suppose,' conceded Gemma, rising to her feet. 'Come on, we'd better go. Lots to do.'

Lots to do. Had they? Dan was surprised but didn't show it. Maybe Gemma wanted to discuss what they'd found out in private. He decided to go along with whatever she wanted for the moment. 'Thanks for showing me around, Bob,' he said, holding out his hand.

Bob clasped his hand giving it a firm shake. 'Maybe you could buy one of these. Be great when you go on your travels.'

Dan laughed. 'Not sure it would fit on a plane.'

'Oh, didn't think of that,' said Bob, joining in the laughter.

As Dan and Gemma headed out of

the boat house Bob called after them. 'Oh, I've just remembered something about Bradshaw. He went to a private school. Frankleton School for Boys, if I remember rightly.'

Gemma halted and turned back towards her father. 'And that's important, why?'

Bob scratched his chin. 'Not sure, really. First time I met him he seemed to want to impress that point on me. I gathered that his parents didn't have much money but his uncle not having children wanted the best for his only nephew, so paid for his education. I got the feeling that it was a sort of bribe so that Alan would carry on the tradition of being a chemist. I also got the feeling that he resented being pushed into that particular career.'

'Well, err, not sure it's helpful but thanks,' said Gemma. 'See you later.'

'OK,' said Bob, walking back towards his work bench and studying the different tins of varnish on display.

'Come on,' said Gemma, grabbing

hold of Dan's hand and pulling him out into the street.

'Where are we going?'

'Lunch. I fancy some fish and chips.'

'I thought we had lots to do.'

'An army marches on its stomach. Food first, then we plan.'

Dan's stomach rumbled at the thought of food. It had been ages since he'd eaten breakfast apart from the slice of cake in the café.

'Lead the way,' he said, his mouth lifting in a smile. He liked the way Gemma's mind worked.

★   ★   ★

They decided to eat alfresco and found a sheltered seating area along the seafront to avoid greedy seagulls looking for their own lunch.

'So what do you think?' asked Gemma, prodding a chip with her wooden fork before popping it into her mouth.

'I think these are the best fish and

chips I've ever tasted.'

'That's not what I . . . ' she began but then looked at his teasing smile. She nudged her elbow into his side. 'I'm being serious.'

'Sorry, couldn't resist. I know you were being serious but sometimes you need to lighten up. Ease the tension, if you know what I mean . . . '

Gemma nodded. She knew exactly what he meant and agreed with what he said but that still didn't stop her wanting to solve the problem in front of them.

'OK, and I agree with you. The best fish and chips ever.'

They gazed out to sea, watching the white crested waves crashing against the wall of the pier, a cold spray dispersing along the promenade. A family passed by, two young children were carrying kites heading towards the vast expanse of sand at the other end of the pier. It prompted a childhood memory of Gemma's. She'd loved the way she could run with her kit trailing behind her until a gust of wind caught the fragile material and sent it swiftly into the air to dance patterns in the sky.

'I'm going to do that again someday.'

'Do what?'

She turned to Dan and realised that she uttered the word out loud. She nodded towards the children. 'Fly a kite on the beach.'

'Sounds like fun,' he said, wiping his mouth with a napkin.

They were both quiet while finishing off their meal and watching the kites.

'So, what's next?' he asked, returning from disposing of the chip wrappings.

Gemma was just about to answer when her mobile rang. Pulling it out of her pocket, she frowned, not recognising the number.

'Hello.'

'Hi, Gemma. It's Hayley.'

'Oh, hi Hayley,' said Gemma.

On hearing Hayley's named mentioned, Dan raised an enquiring eyebrow. Gemma shrugged having no idea why Hayley was calling her.

'Err, I just thought I'd give you a ring. You know, you said if ever I thought of something that would help you contact Penny to let you know. Well, I'm not sure it will be of any use, and it's not something I've thought of, it's more something I've overheard.'

Gemma tried not to sigh but she wished Hayley would get on with it.

'You've heard something?' Gemma prompted.

'Oh yeah. It was when I went out this morning. Well, it was more when I got back.' Gemma heard Hayley take a deep breath before continuing. 'Mr Bradshaw decided he fancied a meringue this morning. Not keen on them myself, bit too gooey for my liking but it's another of his favourites.'

This time Gemma did sigh, sharing Alan Bradshaw's dietary likes or dislikes was not something she was interested in.

'Anyway, when I got back to the shop, the door to the office was open and I heard Mr Bradshaw on the telephone. Nothing unusual in that. I was just going to walk in to give him his meringue when I heard it. Stopped me in my tracks, it did.'

Gemma stiffened. 'What stopped you in your tracks, Hayley?'

'He mentioned Penny's boyfriend's name.'

Gemma's hand tightened around her mobile. 'Oh really. What did he say?'

'Well, that was the odd thing. He said, 'I told you to leave Brian Jackson and that girlfriend of his to me. We should have left the invitation open for a little longer.' He didn't sound happy though, more angry. Strange that — why would you be angry at an invitation?'

'No idea. So, was that all he said?' asked Gemma, trying to sound casual and keep the excitement out of her voice. She could see Dan listening intently to her side of the conversation.

'Near enough, apart from saying that he would meet the caller in Brighton tomorrow afternoon at three o'clock by the Brighton Dome. They'd decide what to do then. Anyway, as I say, it's probably nothing.'

'Oh right, well thanks Hayley. You're probably right. Nothing to worry about.' Gemma didn't believe a word of what she'd just said but didn't want Hayley to know that.

'Well OK. Bye, then.'

Gemma turned off her phone and put it back in her pocket before relating the conversation back to Dan.

'Interesting,' was his only comment.

'Interesting? Is that all you've got to say,' said Gemma, pushing herself up from the bench and standing over him. 'It's the best lead we have and you know it.'

Dan didn't reply, just looked towards the open sea. He appeared to be lost in thought.

'Well?' she said, after the silence went on for far too long.

He turned to look at her, those blue eyes sparkling. 'Looks as though we are off to Brighton tomorrow.'

She reached out a hand and high-fived him. 'Now we're getting somewhere.'

9

The wind whipped around Gemma's hair as she stepped out of the car the next morning. She tucked stray strands under her hat and looked up to see Dan walking out of The Ship.

'Ready?' she said, noticing he'd wrapped up warm in jeans, a thick sweater and jacket.

'Ready. Let's get going boss,' he said, standing to attention and giving her a salute.

'Idiot,' she said, laughing at his actions. 'Come on, before I change my mind and go inside and find the real Dan.'

He clicked his heels. 'Yes Ma'am,' he said in the worst American accent she'd ever heard.

'It really is good of your father to lend us his car again,' said Dan, as he slid into the passenger seat and reached for his seat belt. 'Maybe I should hire one, if I'm going to spend some time around the area. I usually do that if I'm in one place for more than a few days. Never bothered to buy one. No need living in London. Taking the train or tube seems the easiest way to travel.'

Gemma gave him a quick glance before turning on the engine and steering the car into the line of traffic. She agreed with him. She'd given up her own car when she moved to the big city. It seemed such a waste when there were such good travel links in most suburbs.

'Oh, I forgot to mention with all the excitement yesterday about my news.'

'News. What news?'

'Well, you know I delayed my return until yesterday because I met up with my editor.'

Gemma nodded, keeping her eyes on the traffic in front of her.

'Anyway, you gave me an idea and after I tossed it around in my head I decide to pitch it.'

'My idea?' asked Gemma, unsure what possible idea she'd given him for a travel article.

'Folly's,' he said. 'You said how the original was built and it got me wondering how many others there are around this area and the history behind them. Sounded like a good idea and my editor agreed with me.'

'That's great,' said Gemma, taking her eyes off the traffic to give him a quick smile.

'Yes, I thought so, too.' He frowned. 'I only hope we sort this little problem out before too long.' He drummed his fingers on the dashboard. Gemma saw his shoulders tense. Brian's disappearance must be wearing him down. She hadn't realised until that moment that it was worst for him. Not knowing where his only living relative was must be constantly on his mind.

She kept quiet, giving no response just concentrating on manoeuvring the car onto the main road out of Westlea

Bay and towards Brighton.

'How about we play tourists for this morning. Give us a break from worrying about Brian and Penny,' she said, not wanting the silence to continue. 'We have plenty of time.'

Dan considered it for a moment before nodding his head. 'OK, sounds like a good idea. Anything of interest spring to mind?'

Gemma tapped a finger on her lips. 'How about the long man?'

'Long man?'

'Locally known as the Wilmington Giant. It's a chalk figure cut into the hill and can be seen for miles around. It was thought be have originated from the iron age, but later investigation claims that it may have been as late as the 16th or 17th century. Anyway, fancy a visit?'

Dan relaxed his shoulders. 'Sounds interesting. Lead the way.'

The traffic was light and they made good progress towards Wilmington. Gemma pointed out local landmarks that she thought might be of interest to him.

Dan explained that he usually carried his camera everywhere, taking pictures of anything that he thought would be of interest to his readers. Sometimes, after some research, items were discarded as not good enough. Others he would research deeper until he was satisfied that they could be included in a future article.

'There you go,' said Gemma as the Tall Man came into view. 'What do you think?'

Dan looked at the figure carved into the hill. Standing straight and tall, arms outstretched, holding two staves.

'Impressive.'

Gemma followed the signs to the car park. It appeared to be a quiet day for visitors and there were plenty of spaces available.

'Ready for a walk?' she said, turning off the engine and releasing her seat belt. She reached for a scarf that was lying on the back seat and wrapped it around her neck. For good measure she reached into her pockets and pulled out a pair of gloves. She saw Dan raise an eyebrow.

'We can walk to the top and it's going to get cold,' she said, pulling her hat further down around her ears. 'Hope you're fit.' She opened the door and stepped outside into the cold wind.

Dan stepped out of the car and zipped up his jacket. 'We'll see whose fit,' he said, stepping around the car and grabbing hold of her hand, pulling her along towards the entrance to the pathways. His pace was fast and Gemma's steps turned into a jog to keep up with him.

'Hey, not so fast,' she said, tugging against his grip on her hand.

He gave a carefree laugh and carried on tugging her along. 'Now who's not fit?'

She shrugged and said nothing. She was getting to like this carefree Dan but she knew she should put a stop to her growing attraction.

As they climbed further the figure became more impressive. He pulled out his mobile phone.

'This will have to do. Not perfect but never mind.' He snapped away on his phone, taking more pictures the larger the etching became.

'It's incredible,' remarked Dan as they reached the top. 'The images these people created is awesome. And just look at that view.'

They scanned the view before them. The only sound, the wind gusting around them. Gemma shivered and wrapped her arms around her body. There were spots of rain in the air and looking up into the sky she detected darkened clouds hovering above.

'Come on, let's go back. If we head to the motorway we'll be in Brighton in half an hour. We can do a bit more sightseeing before heading towards the Dome.'

The threatening rain turned into a slow drizzle as they made their way down the hill and they only just made it to the car before a heavy shower fell around them.

'How about some lunch?' she said, turning up the heating and welcoming the warmth as it quickly spread through the car.

'Great. All that walking has given me an appetite,' he grinned.

'Brighton's quite a popular resort. There are some great places to eat. Ever been?'

Dan shook his head. 'It's strange. I'm a travel writer. You'd think I would visit my own country before exploring others.'

'I think most people are like that. You know? Never looking at the good points that are in their own back yard.'

Dan nodded in agreement. 'You're probably right. Never thought about it like that. With me it's always been the idea that there's something more incredible across the sea.'

'I remember once,' said Gemma, 'when I was working in the shop. A tourist came in to buy something or other. It was one of those awful summers. Rainy days, continually overcast. I got the feeling she'd only come inside to get out of a particularly bad storm. We got talking. She remarked how wonderful she found Westlea Bay. She was from Spain, if I remember rightly. I remarked that she was lucky coming from such a hot country where you could guarantee good summer weather. Do you know what she said?'

Dan shook his head.

'But you have wonderful green countryside. Appreciate what you have and don't be envious of others.'

Dan looked out of the window at the green fields. 'She was right. We do have some great countryside. We've just seen it from the top of that hill. Thanks for pointing that out to me.' He held up his hand and with his forefinger began writing an imaginary note. 'Must include more travel articles from within own country.' He dropped is hand. 'There, noted.'

'A good plan,' said Gemma, chuckling before taking the slip road to the motorway and pressing down on the accelerator.

★   ★   ★

Deciding to eat before arriving in Brighton, they found a village just off the motorway. The blackboard menu displayed outside offered a wide variety of fare and Gemma pulled into the car park.

'Come on,' she said, rubbing her hands together. 'I don't know about you, but I could do with a cup of coffee.'

Dan nodded and they made their way into the pub. There was a small lounge area to the side with a blazing fire that looked so inviting that Gemma headed straight for the warmth. The pub wasn't busy. The bad weather had obviously deterred passing traffic and only a few locals hung around the bar area. She removed her hat and shrugged off her jacket and began warming her hands. Dan walked up to the bar and ordered a couple of cups of coffee. He studied a menu while being served before tucking it under his arm and picking up the steaming cups.

'OK, let's see what they have to offer,' he said as he placed the mugs on the table and handed Gemma a menu. He pulled out his glasses from his pocket and pushed them on. 'The homemade steak and kidney pudding looks good,' he said after a moment of studying what was on offer. 'How about you?'

'Sounds good to me,' said Gemma, putting down her menu and wrapping her hands around her cup of coffee before taking a sip. She closed her eyes, savouring the taste and fragrance of the brew. She opened her eyes to see Dan had gone to order their food. He was leaning against the bar, laughing at something the barman was saying and, as if sensing her eyes were on him, he turned and their gazes locked for a moment. Gemma was the first to turn away, pretending to look for something in her handbag.

'They'll bring the food over when it's ready,' said Dan, settling back down in his seat.

Gemma nodded but said nothing, still a little embarrassed about what had just happened.

She pulled out a tissue from her bag and wiped her nose.

Dan said nothing for a moment, just studied her face.

'Something wrong?' she asked when the silence seemed to stretch out a little too long.

'Can I ask you something personal?' he said.

Gemma shrugged, wondering what he wanted to know. 'Sure, go ahead. I'll let you know if you cross the line.'

He paused for a moment.

'Dan,' she prompted.

'Sorry,' he said and she sensed he was struggling to find the right words. 'It's just that sometimes you have a faraway look in your eyes and you look as though you've been hurt. Has someone hurt you, Gemma?'

Gemma looked at him in surprise, her face burning with embarrassment at him being so perceptive. Should she tell him about Robbie? Would he think her foolish? She considered brushing off his words but then thought again. She might as well confess. After all, they probably wouldn't see each other after they found Brian and Penny.

She gave a weak smile and shifted in her seat, wondering where to start.

Dan stayed silent, those blue eyes studying her face, waiting for her to tell her tale.

'Can we eat first, Dan?' she asked as she saw a young girl approach carrying two plates of steaming food.

She gave a sigh of relief as Dan nodded. Another few minutes of reprieve before she related how foolish she'd once been.

The conversation was kept to light topics as the meal progressed. Favourite films, books they enjoyed reading. Gemma began to relax a little although the up and coming subject was never far from her mind.

Dan scraped the last of his meal onto his fork and popped it into his mouth. 'That was absolutely delicious,' he said, after a moment.

Gemma agreed, surprised to see that she'd managed to eat every last crumb.

'Another cup of coffee,' said Dan, 'or do you fancy a glass of wine?'

'I'm driving, remember. Coffee is great.'

She watched him as he went to order the drinks. She hated talking about this episode in her life. She felt such a fool. Her eyes began to water and she swallowed to regain her composure.

'Hey,' said Dan, as he placed their drinks on the table. 'Whatever it is, it can't be that bad.' He reached out and thumbed a tear away from her cheek. The tenderness in those blue eyes made something in Gemma's stomach flip and she took a deep gulp of breath.

'Have you ever wondered why I moved to London?' she asked.

Dan shrugged. 'Not really, just assumed it was because of your work.'

'I'm an illustrator, Dan. I can work anywhere. Give me pencils, paper and something to draw and I'm away. I could have stayed at home.'

'So why didn't you?'

'The obvious. I met someone. Robbie the Rat to be precise.' She shuddered, even speaking his name unsettled her.

Dan raised an eyebrow but said nothing.

She reached for her cup and took a sip.

'I'd just finished university and was working in the gift shop before deciding what I wanted to do with my art degree.

'Some friends who worked at a local hotel were having a beach party and invited me along. Robbie was staying at the hotel and was invited along as well. He was good looking. He asked me out and I said yes.'

She paused for a moment, lost in her own thoughts.

'Go on,' prompted Dan.

'Robbie worked for the hotel chain. He was here for the summer assessing the workings of the hotel and seeing if there could be improvements made. As the summer progressed we became closer and the date for his departure was on the horizon. His main base was at the head office in London. He suggested I move there to be near him. By then my illustrations had begun to sell and I could see a future for my art work.

'I thought he wanted me to move in with him. I should have known something was wrong when he insisted that wasn't a good idea and it would be better if I found a place of my own.' She gave a wry smile. 'It's true what they say — love is blind. So I went along with it. Found a flat I could afford with a little help from my parents and moved away from home. The dream romance lasted three weeks.'

157

'Three weeks?' said Dan, reaching out and giving her hand a reassuring squeeze. Gemma attempted to pull away from of his grasp but he held on.

'We hadn't arrange to meet that morning but I'd just received a new commission, bigger than normal. I was so excited I decided to go round to Robbie's office and surprise him with the news. Thought I'd take him out for a celebratory lunch.' She gave a short laugh. 'Stupid me. When I asked the receptionist if I could speak to him, do you know what she said?'

Dan shrugged.

'Sorry, you've just missed him. He's taken his fiancée out to lunch.' She felt the strength of Dan's hands wrapped around her own giving her reassurance. 'Turned out she was the boss's daughter. I felt such a fool. I never guessed. Couldn't even understand why he would want me to move to London. Surely he would know that I'd find out eventually.'

Dan said nothing for a moment,

taking in all the signs of hurt crossing Gemma's face. 'So, what did you do?'

Gemma sighed. 'Cut all ties. Refused to answer his calls. He came around to the flat a couple of times but I never answered the door. In the end I just got on with my life. A little bit older but a whole lot wiser.'

She leant back in her chair, surprised how relieved she was about retelling her sorry story.

'So are you over the betrayal?'

'Well, let's put it like this, I'm not ready to go into another relationship just yet. The issue is trust, Dan. If you can't have trust between two people, what have you got?'

Dan released her hand and picked up his pint glass draining the contents. He looked at her for a long moment before reaching out once more for her hand. 'I promise you Gemma, you can trust me. Whatever I do, I will never let you down like your ex.'

'How can I be sure?'

Dan crossed his arms across his chest

and those piercing blue eyes took hold of her gaze once more. 'That's something you have to decide for yourself. Do you think you can trust me?'

Could she? Could she take the gamble again? Something moved within her, a shift of something she'd been holding onto seemed to slip away into the past. She gave him a weak smile. 'I think so. Just don't ever lie to me, Dan.'

'I promise never to do anything that will hurt you in the long run. OK?' He looked into her eyes.

'That's all I ask.' She gave a deep sigh and pushed back her chair. 'Come on, let's forget all about my stupid decisions in the past and get on with the real problem in front of us.'

'Fine by me. Let's go and catch the baddies.'

10

The tension eased from Gemma as they headed towards Brighton. She explained about her latest idea for a set of drawings connected with the sea. She'd developed the idea in her head after watching her mother collect the shells from the beach. The shapes, the colours, small and large. She might even include coral, but, of course, for that she would have to travel.

'If I'm honest, I'm just a little bit jealous of my parents. Heading off, the camper taking them onto foreign soil.' She sighed. 'I'll do it one day. Just put a pin in a map of the world and see where it sends me.'

'You never know, it might happen sooner than later,' he replied.

Gemma gave him a quick glance. 'Maybe, but at the moment it's just a distant dream.'

161

'That's what I thought when I first decided on being a travel writer.' He raised both his hands and spread them wide. 'But here I am — proof that dreams do come true.'

'OK, I'll hold onto my dream. Just in case.'

As they approached Brighton their chatter ceased. The traffic began to build up and Gemma concentrated on the road while Dan looked for directions to the Dome and a parking area. It took longer than they thought and by the time they'd managed to find an empty spot in the almost full car park, it was nearly time for them to find out who Bradshaw was meeting.

'You know, I don't know if we'll find him in this crowd,' said Gemma, stepping off the pavement to avoid bumping into a couple of children coming towards them. 'I forgot how big this place is.' She looked down the road towards the entrance of the Dome. 'Oh, look,' she said, recognising someone across the road. 'Isn't that the chap that you were giving directions to at the station?'

She felt him stiffen beside her and gave him a curious look but nothing showed on his face.

He shrugged. 'Must have decided to move down the coast.' He turned his attention back to the entrance of the Dome.

'Keep your eyes open and hopefully we'll see Bradshaw. It's a pity Hayley didn't hear the whereabouts of where exactly at the Dome Bradshaw planned to have his meeting,' said Dan, grabbing hold of Gemma's hand and guiding her back onto the pavement.

He'd read up about the Brighton Dome on the internet the night before, with its many art events being carried out during the year. Even in the autumn months the place was busy.

Gemma stopped suddenly and let go of his hand. 'Look, is that him?' she said, pointing towards the entrance.

Dan looked ahead to where she was indicating. Sure enough, just past the entrance stood Bradshaw. They watched him as he looked up and down the street before deciding to cross the road away from the Dome.

'Where's he going?' asked Gemma.

'Nowhere, by the looks of it,' said Dan, as he watched Bradshaw looking up and down the street at the passing traffic before walking in the other direction.

'Come on, Dan. He's on the move. We don't want to lose sight of him.'

The crowd was still thick and Dan had trouble keeping Bradshaw in sight, luckily he was tall enough to see over most people but the distance between them seemed to be lengthening.

He watched as Bradshaw quickly dodged into a street ahead. A dark coloured car made the same turning a moment later.

'Hurry,' said Dan, grabbing Gemma's hand and tugging her along. 'We're going to lose him.'

It was too late. By the time they made the turning Bradshaw was at the top of the road and stepping into the car.

'Oh no,' cried Gemma, as the passenger door slammed shut and the car took off, disappearing out of sight.

Dan stopped walking and ran a hand through his hair in frustration.

'Did you recognise the car, Gemma?'

'Sorry, no,' she said, shoulders slumped as she looked straight ahead. 'Couldn't even get the registration. It was too far away. Did you?'

He shook his head. They seemed to be so near to finding out answers and now it was swiftly taken away from them.

'Well, I suppose we're a bit further forward.'

Gemma looked at him, opened mouthed. 'Really. How do you reckon that?'

'Well, we're now looking for a black saloon car. That, at least, I recognised.'

'Fat lot of good that is,' she said, turning back towards the way they came. 'You do know how many of that type of vehicle are in this country?'

'Well, no, but I'm sure there's a lot,' he said.

She looked so defeated he put his arm around her shoulder and gave it a comforting squeeze.

'Come on, let's take a walk along the pier and decide what to do next.'

It seemed to Dan that all he'd looked at over the last few days was a large expanse of grey, angry sea with seagulls ducking, diving and squawking above him. He could see a hint of blue in the sky above and hoped, at last, that the weather was turning for the better.

He looked across at Gemma as she huddled down into her jacket, her woolly hat covering her ash blonde hair. She'd said nothing since they'd lost sight of Alan Bradshaw. He could understand how she felt. He really thought they were getting somewhere when they headed towards Brighton this morning.

'Come on,' he said, taking hold of Gemma's elbow. 'We need cheering up.'

'Where are we going?' she asked as he tugged her along the promenade towards a concession stand ahead of them.

'We need candy floss.'

'What?' said Gemma, looking at him as though he'd lost his senses.

'When I was a kid, candy floss was always a treat when we went on holiday,' he explained. 'My dad used to say that it was better than medicine.' He grinned, remembering, with fondness, his father's words. 'I remember once we were on the beach. I was about five and Brian was a baby. Dad and I decided to build a sandcastle. We spent hours on it, digging the foundations, steps up to a gateway, four turrets and a moat surrounding it.' He paused for a moment looking at the sand where it met the sea. There were no sand castles on the beach today. 'Anyway, after what seemed like hours we sat back admiring our efforts. To me it was all my adventures rolled into one. I was a knight who would defend the castle for the king. I would ride my horse and fight in many battles. Then it happened.'

Gemma put her hand to her mouth. 'Oh no, what happened?'

'Some older kids were playing football nearby. The ball was kicked extra hard straight onto my castle. The kid chasing it down didn't stop in time and slid straight into my creation, destroying it.' He shrugged. 'I'm ashamed to say, I cried.'

Gemma looked at him with sympathy. 'I'd have done the same. After all that hard work. So what happened then?'

'Dad picked me up and put me on his shoulders and said he knew just the thing to make it better.'

'Let me guess — candy floss?'

Dan nodded. 'You know that was the best tasting candy floss I ever had and as Dad and I walked along the beach with our treat he said we could build an even better castle the next day.'

'And did you?'

'You bet. Come on, let's go and buy some. Makes everyone feel better even if it's just for a short while.'

He let go of her elbow and took her gloved hand in his and led her to the brightly coloured stand.

★ ★ ★

'So where do we go from here?' asked Gemma, as they walked along the seafront, munching on the pink, fluffy confectionary. 'You know, this does taste good.'

Dan grinned. 'Told you it would make you feel better.' He pulled off a piece and popped it in his mouth. He closed his eyes, savouring the sugary treat as it melted on his tongue. He opened his eyes to see Gemma looking at him. She was grinning and at least, for a moment, he'd put a smile back on her face.

'OK,' he said. 'Well, whatever has happened to Brian and Penny, I'm sure they're still OK.'

Gemma looked at him in alarm. 'Oh lord, you don't think . . . '

Dan raised a hand immediately knowing what her thoughts were. 'No, nothing like that. Well, I must confess a couple of times something along those lines did go through my mind but after hearing what Hayley overheard Bradshaw saying, I dismissed that idea.'

He watched Gemma relax a little.

'Sorry, didn't mean to frighten you.'

'I suppose we should face the fact that something bad could have happened to them.'

Dan shook his head. 'No, let's stay positive. Whatever has happened we're both sure that it has something to do with Bradshaw and Norton. Now, whether Tovey has anything to do with it, I'm not too sure at the moment. We need to get a look inside the folly. What that building has to do with it I am at a loss to understand but I'm almost sure there will be some sort of clue hidden inside. Do you think we can take a look tonight?'

Gemma was quiet for a moment.

'I'd rather try in the daylight. Dad was telling me this morning that this latest storm caused a few rock falls a few miles up the coast. Going at night-time is too dangerous.'

Dan could see the sense in this.

'OK, tomorrow morning then. Hopefully we can get in without Tovey or Norton spotting us.'

'Yes, let's hope so.'

Dan checked his watch. 'I suppose we should head back.'

They finished their candy floss and began walking back towards the car park.

'We could or we could do something else.'

'Like what?'

Gemma nibbled on her lip. 'I know men don't usually like doing this . . . '

'Doing what?' he asked, wondering what on earth she was talking about.

'Shopping,' she said. 'Well to be more precise, window shopping.'

'Shopping. Why do woman always

think that men are adverse to that particular art?' He stood back and pushed his hands in his pockets.

'Oh, I don't know. Maybe because most of my previous boyfriend's would rather walk over hot coals than accompany me on a shopping trip.'

'Well, I'm not most men. Come on, lead the way to my doom.' He gave her an exaggerated look of horror which made her laugh.

'OK, only an hour, I promise. Let's head towards The Lanes.'

'The Lanes?'

'Narrow lanes, loads of small retail outlets, eateries, cafés. They sell everything. Jewellery, clothes, watches. Almost everything you can think of.' She pulled up suddenly and looked at him. 'You know, a travel article about Brighton would be great. There is so much you can do.'

Dan looked around him and agreed. Even on a cold day, the whole area seemed to bustle with people. He'd make a note to explore further and see if it was viable or not.

Gemma started walking again. 'Come on, I doubt I'll buy anything but window shopping is good for any girl.'

Dan shook his head and said nothing, just falling into step beside her.

The Lanes was as good as Gemma described and Dan thought it was an area that he would definitely write about. Hidden away, it was a revelation of good shopping and the atmosphere was fantastic.

'Thanks for bringing me,' he said as he followed behind Gemma along a particularly narrow lane and bumped into her as she stopped to look into a shop window.

'Great, isn't it?' she said, bending down to look at a piece of antique jewellery. 'I'm just going to go inside here and take a closer look at the brooches. Mum's birthday is coming up soon and it looks as though they have some lovely pieces from the Victorian era.'

'Not planning to buy anything? Should have known a woman couldn't resist.' He chuckled as she gave him a 'what did you expect' look.

'There's an art shop just up ahead. I'll window shop up there and wait for you.'

She nodded and disappeared into the shop.

Dan moved along towards the art shop and pulled out his phone and dialled a number.

'No good,' he said. 'Bradshaw got into a car. Didn't see who was picking him up.' He listened for a moment. 'No, I'm positive she's not involved but I'm sure she'll lead me to who is.' He paused for a moment. 'No, she doesn't know what I know and at the moment I'm reluctant to tell her. Safer if I'm the only one with the knowledge.' He turned back and saw Gemma coming out of the shop. 'I have to go, speak to you later.'

He shoved his phone back in his pocket. Only a few hours ago he'd told

Gemma that she could trust him. He only hoped once she discovered what he was doing that she would be forgiving. For some reason it was important to him.

★ ★ ★

After an hour of browsing they decided to head back to Westlea Bay. They stopped once when Gemma received a call from a customer. The recent artwork she had sent them wasn't quite right and they wanted immediate alterations.

'Bother,' she said, tucking her phone back in her pocket and pulling out of the lay-by. 'It'll take me all evening to sort it.'

They'd talked about going out for a meal.

'Sorry, I'll have to cancel. I wouldn't bother but they are an important client and I don't want to lose them.'

'No worries. I quite understand having been in that position myself a

number of times. I'll just grab something to eat at The Ship. We'll meet up
tomorrow as planned.'

★ ★ ★

Dan wandered into the bar. Whitey
wasn't in her usual spot behind the bar,
instead a young man who just about
passed the minimum drinking age
served him with a pint. It felt a bit like
déjà vu as he looked around. The two
sailors sat in the same spot he'd seen
them last. It looked as though their ship
was still awaiting repairs. There was no
young man — he must have booked out
after his interview. His gaze drifted to
the corner where the two old men
usually resided. The dominoes were out
on the table, all laid out ready to play
but there was only Reg sat at the table.
Dan picked up his pint and walked
over.

'No partner tonight?' he said indicating to the empty seat.

'Bill's daughter's birthday. They've

176

gone out for a meal.' He looked at Dan as though it was forbidden to miss out on a game of dominoes.

'Ah,' said Dan, in complete understanding. 'Do you know, I haven't played for years. Can I join you? The name's Dan, by the way.'

Reg nodded towards the empty seat and began shuffling the dominoes. Half an hour later Dan admitted to himself that his opponent was a master player having won the last three games. He leant back in his chair and rubbed a hand across his chin.

'You're just too good,' he said, draining his beer and holding up his glass. 'Fancy another?'

'Just a half, thanks,' said Reg, pushing his glass towards Dan.

Waiting for the drinks to be poured, the door to the bar opened. Dan idly looked round and was surprised to see Alan Bradshaw and Ian Norton walk in. Norton gave him a nod of recognition before taking a seat next to the two sailors while Bradshaw approached the

177

bar. Dan paid for his own drinks and wandered back over to Reg who'd already shuffled the dominoes for the next game.

'So, Reg. How long have you lived around here?' asked Dan, hoping that his playing partner would be happy to indulge in a little local gossip.

'Born and bred,' said Reg, taking a healthy swallow from his glass.

'Bet you've seen some changes?'

'That I have. Place was only a small seaside resort when I was a kid. Now, since they built a couple of big hotels just off the seafront the place is like Piccadilly Circus. Look at this place, used to be one of the busiest in the area but Whitey can't compete with those big hotel chains.'

'What about Westlea Manor? Going to be a conference centre, isn't it?'

'Oh, so you've heard that rumour, have you?'

'Rumour? I thought it was going ahead. Been given council approval.'

Reg said nothing for a moment and

Dan wondered that maybe he'd asked too much. 'Well, with the likes of him in charge,' he said, nodding towards Ian Norton, 'it'll never get done. Not even started on sprucing it up, so I've heard.' He leant forward in his chair and whispered. 'And that boss of his, Tovey, doesn't seem to be making any headway. Not sure what they're playing at but it sure isn't developing a so-called conference centre.'

'Really,' said Dan, thinking what a useful mine of information Reg was.

'So what do you think they're up to then?'

'Not worked it out yet, but something's going on. Take his mate, over there.' He lowered his voice even more forcing Dan to move a little closer to hear him. 'He's another strange one. Came here after his uncle died and took over the family chemist shop.'

Dan nodded not letting on that he already knew this detail.

'How he ever became a pharmacist is beyond me. Used to have a market stall somewhere around London way. Sold cosmetics and stuff like that. You tell me, how does a bloke go from being a market trader to making up prescriptions?'

'Well he'd have to have qualified, he wouldn't be allowed to do his job otherwise,' Dan replied.

'Suppose,' conceded Reg. 'Then that Norton fella appears, turns out he and his mate over there went to school together. Got expelled too.'

Dan raised an eyebrow. Interesting, he'd not heard that little titbit before.

Reg must have seen his reaction. 'Overheard the pair of them talking one night. Not that I was listening, like,' he hastened to add.

'Of course not,' Dan reassured him.

'They were talking at the bar while I was waiting for my pint. The barrel was empty and Whitey went to tap a new one. They were laughing about some stunt they'd pulled at school along with another chap. Not sure what it was but it must have been serious for the school to take the action they did.'

'Must have been,' agreed Dan. 'Wonder what school that was?'

Reg scratched his chin. 'Funny name if I remember rightly. Reminded me of a vegetable.'

'Carrot? Cauliflower?'

Reg chortled. 'Never heard of Carrot College.' He tapped his forehead and frowned before pointing a finger at Dan. 'Kale College. That's what it was called. Anyway, not long after Norton arrived, his boss, Tovey appeared and bought the Manor. Made all sorts of promises. Not one carried out so far.' He sniffed, a look of disgust crossing his face. He straightened himself in his chair and gave the dominoes another shuffle.

'One more game?'

Dan grinned. 'OK, think I can manage one more beating.'

'Practice, son. It just takes practice.' He winked and Dan burst out laughing.

Reg easily won the next game and draining the last of his drink, stood up and said goodnight.

Dan sat back in his chair and went over the information he'd discovered. The connections were, slowly coming together. What they meant, he wasn't sure, but he intended to find out. He looked over to the group in the corner. Their voices were low as they talked among themselves. Even straining his ears he couldn't hear what they were saying. After about five minutes Norton stood up and left. Bradshaw followed not long after, leaving Dan and the two sailors the only occupants of the bar. He finished his own pint and watched as the sailors also stood up and left the bar.

Dan took his empty glass to the bar and checked his watch. For some reason he felt restless and decided to take a walk along the seafront before bed. He headed towards his bedroom to collect a warm jacket. The two sailors were opening the door to one of the other rooms. He nodded to them and went on his way. He sensed them staring at him and wondered why he felt uncomfortable?

*   *   *

He walked outside, pulled the collar of his jacket up around his neck and shoved his hands in his pockets. Trying to decide which direction to go in he looked up and down the road. He could see a figure further in the distance and recognised Alan Bradshaw. He was talking to someone in the shadows and Dan decided to walk in that direction. Bradshaw must have heard him approaching and looked up. He uttered something and strode quickly out of sight. Dan picked up his pace hoping to see who Bradshaw was talking to. He was unlucky. Whoever it was disappeared into the night. He heard a noise, something he was sure he'd heard before, but couldn't quite capture in his mind. Never mind it would come to him.

He walked along the seafront. He

could see the lights from the broken ship in the distance and wondered how long it would be before it went on its way. It must be losing money not being able to deliver its cargo. Oh well, none of his business. He'd other urgent matters to attend to. Hopefully, tomorrow, the folly would reveal its secrets.

11

Gemma hurried along the pathway. She'd received a text from Dan the night before. He'd picked up some interesting information but didn't elaborate, much to her annoyance. He said he'd meet her at the bottom of the walkway to the cliffs the next morning and reveal everything.

Luck appeared to be going their way as the sea was calm and the wind dying down to an autumn breeze. She could see Dan up ahead. He was talking on his phone. No surprise there. His free hand was threaded through his hair, a look of frustration crossing his features. As if sensing her approach he finished his call and tucked away his mobile.

She didn't bother to ask him who he was talking to. He'd only say his editor or some other work related nonsense. Gemma was sure he was keeping something from her. Could she trust him? He said she could. She brushed away the negative thoughts and concentrated on more immediate matters.

'So, tell me what your news is?' she asked, as she came to his side. Dan shook his head. 'Didn't I tell you to be patient?'

'If I'm any more patient I'll combust,' she said, feeling just a little bit irritated.

He held up his hands in a gesture of defence. 'OK. Calm down. I'll tell you on the way.'

As they strode up the path, Gemma listened as he revealed the information he'd learnt the night before. At last they were getting somewhere.

'So that's how they know each other? You know what this means, Dan?'

'We have a connection.'

'Exactly. I wish we could find out what they were expelled for,' said Gemma, 'although I doubt it is important.'

'I suppose so. Anyway, for the time being let's concentrate on getting into the folly without being seen. I'm positive we will find some answers once we get inside the building.'

'Hopefully Tovey or Norton won't be looking out for us this time. Just to be on the safe side if we go further along the pathway we can take another route and approach from the other side of the copse which will give us some cover.'

'Great idea,' said Dan, letting Gemma lead the way.

'It gets a bit tricky up ahead,' said Gemma, as they passed the gate they'd used on their first visit. 'The pathway narrows and slopes down towards the cliff edge so we'll have to go along in single file. Watch your step. It can get slippery.'

Gemma was right, the rain from the storm made manoeuvring along the path difficult and a couple of times she lost her footing and felt Dan's hand reaching out to steady her. Her legs brushed against the gorse that grew in large clumps along the pathway and she breathed in the smell of coconuts that the leaves emitted into the air.

Finally the path began to meander inwards away from the cliff top and the ground became firmer under foot.

'OK, we're nearly there,' she said. 'Just up ahead, along that hedge line there's a gap. It's a bit narrow but you should be able to squeeze through.'

'I hope you're not inferring that I'm fat,' he said, raising an eyebrow.

She shook her head. 'Not at all. I was just thinking maybe your broad shoulders wouldn't be able to push through the gap,' she said, tongue in cheek.

'Broad shoulders? Thanks for noticing.'

Gemma rolled her eyes but said nothing. She pushed herself through the gap and watched Dan follow her with some difficulty as the branches tried to hold him back.

'You were right,' he said, brushing away a few twigs and leaves from his clothes, 'a tight squeeze.'

'Come on. We'd better hurry.'

The roof and top floor of Westlea

Manor could be seen just above the hill in the distance.

'Dad was right,' she mused. 'It doesn't look as though there is any work being done to the main building.'

'How can you tell? Could be Tovey is doing internal work first.'

'Maybe, but I'm sure Dad mentioned that the roof needed a lot of work. Something about it leaking. Can't see any scaffolding erected.'

Dan said nothing for a moment just staring at the building. 'Come on, let's check out the folly before someone finds out what we're up to.'

They walked along the edge of the copse until the folly came into view. Dan pulled out a pair of small cutters from his inside jacket pocket.

Gemma looked down and raised an eyebrow.

'To cut through the wire,' he said by way of explanation. 'Went to the hardware store before meeting you.' He held them up in the air. 'Come on, let's go exploring.'

Coming from a different direction they approached the back of the folly. From the back it was a flat building.

'I thought the whole building would be circular,' observed Dan.

'A bit of an illusion I'm afraid. Only the front appears that way.'

'I'll tackle the barbed wire to the left of the building. It's furthest away from the trees and, hopefully, prying eyes.'

He walked over to the fence and began cutting away. The barbed wire was tough to cut through and the implement not the best. After a couple of minutes, a few curses and nicks to the hand, he managed to make a big enough hole for them both to get through.

They walked to the front of the building, climbing the steps to the front door. Gemma turned the door knob and it opened without difficulty.

They stepped inside, closing the door behind them. It was just one large area apart from a curtain hanging on the far right. There was little of interest in the room. The walls were plain with just a couple of rusted picture hooks hanging from a picture rail that ran around the room. An old cane chair lay on its side. Maybe used by the Colonel when he was reading one of his favourite books, thought Gemma. She went to upturn it then decided against it. Things were best left as they were.

Dan inspected a set of drawers pushed up against the wall.

'Anything interesting?' she asked as she watched him pull out one of the drawers.

'Nothing,' he said, shutting the last drawer and wiping dust from his hands. 'Don't think it's been used for years.'

Gemma shoved her hands in her pockets and looked around one more time. 'I really thought we'd find something,' she said, trying to keep the disappointment out of her voice. 'But there's nothing.' She waited for Dan to agree with her but he said nothing. She looked up and found he'd moved away from the drawers and was pulling at the curtain.

'Well, well. What have we here?' he said as the curtain gave way to reveal a door.

'A hidden room, maybe,' said Gemma as she watched Dan twist the door knob, push against the door and disappeared inside.

He returned a moment later. 'Just an old-fashioned pantry, by the looks of it. Nothing interesting.'

'Are you sure?' said Gemma, pushing past him and taking a look herself.

He was right. It was most likely used years ago when the previous owners used the folly. It was completely empty apart from a couple of shelves constructed along the back wall. One of the shelves was broken and only a bracket remained.

'There must be something,' she said, running her hands along one of the shelves and looking underneath as if expecting to see a clue jump out and hit her in the face. She stood still trying not to show the disappointment she felt.

'There's nothing,' said Dan, coming up beside her and putting his arm around her.

She shrugged him off, her anger rising. She knew it wasn't his fault but her worry of Penny and Brian was overtaking her common sense.

'There must be something or why else would Penny mention it?' she said waving her hands about. One of them bumped painfully again the iron bracket on the wall.'

'Ouch,' she said pulling at the bracket in temper. To her surprise the bracket moved easily and she heard a click and a panel to the side began to move.

'A secret door.' She tried to keep the excitement out of her voice. 'I wonder what's behind it?' She peered inside to take a better look. 'Too dark, I can't see anything.'

'Here, let me,' said Dan, pulling his phone out of his pocket and turning it on to give a ray of light. 'Stupid me, I forgot to bring the torches I bought the other day. This will have to do.'

Its light was poor but Gemma followed his idea and pulled out her own phone, the two beams together giving them a better view. A wooden staircase descended into the darkness below but without venturing further they wouldn't be able to see what lay beyond.

'Look, there's a rope rail there. Hold onto that and let's see where it leads. Go carefully and I'll follow behind you.'

She watched him close the door behind him, sealing off the outside world.

'Just in case,' he said. He didn't have to say anything further. Tovey or Norton could turn up at any minute and discover them. Leaving any evidence of a disturbance in the folly would only alert the two men.

Gemma nodded, grabbed hold of the rail and began to slowly descend, gingerly testing the strength of the wooden staircase as she went. It appeared solid and she nodded to Dan to follow her. Down and down they went, which seemed to last forever although Gemma doubted it was more than a couple of minutes until the staircases stopped and she stepped onto solid ground. She held up her mobile phone and looked around her. She could make out a small cave with a passageway leading away from the staircase, a roped rail fitted into the wall.

'I think I know what this is,' said Dan, his voice echoing around the small cave.

'So do I,' said Gemma. 'A smugglers' cave.'

'Unbelievable,' murmured Dan, turning full circle to get a better view of the cave. 'I feel like I've landed a part in the *Treasure Island* novel and there should be a chest of gold hidden around here somewhere.'

Gemma started to laugh but the echo sounded so eerie she stopped.

'Did you know about this place?' he

asked, reaching out and touching the rock wall.

'Not at all. I mean, I know of them. Anyone living on the coast does. There's one the other side of Westlea Bay. It's a big tourist attraction, but it's in the opposite direction from here.'

'Could this,' said Dan, moving towards the passageway, 'lead to that opening?'

Gemma shook her head. 'No, I've explored that one, it's just a couple of passages leading to one large cave with no pathways leading from it.'

Dan grabbed hold of the roped rail. 'Come on, let's see where this leads. Turn your mobile off just in case I run out of battery then we can use yours on the way back.'

The passageway slowly descended and after a couple of minutes another passage came into view, veering off to the left. Dan halted and let go of the rope and, walking over to the entrance, shone the light inside before returning to Gemma.

'Nothing but a smaller cave. Come on, let's keep going.'

They made their way slowly. A couple of times the path broadened out into a large cave but nothing interesting came into view. Whispers of wind curled around the winding path as they ventured further along in the gloomy light. Gemma wondered if any minute they'd bump into a pirate wearing a patch and a tricorn hat. Everything seemed so surreal.

Suddenly Dan stopped causing Gemma to bump into him.

'What the . . . '

'Shhh.' He put a finger to his lips and whispered, 'Listen I think I can hear voices.'

Gemma strained to listen, there were definite mumblings from up ahead. 'Someone's coming.'

Dan shone the light around the passageway which luckily had widened. He couldn't see anything for a moment and then something caught his eye.

'Over there, quick.'

Gemma looked to where he was pointing, six feet off the ground was a ledge. 'Come on we can hide in there, it looks big enough to hold the two of us.'

He pulled Gemma along and helped her up and scrambled in after her. It was deeper than he first thought with just enough room for them both to hide. Dan turned off his phone and darkness descended. The sound of voices began to fill the passageway and a glow of light began to fill the cave. The mumble of voices became clearer and Gemma recognised one of them.

'Norton,' she whispered to Dan and felt him squeeze her hand in acknowledgement.

Three men entered the cave and Dan and Gemma moved as far back as they could to hide from view.

'Keep hold of the rope rail. I don't want either of you wandering off. These tunnels lead off all over the place,' Gemma heard Norton say.

There was a mumble from one of the men but Gemma couldn't understand what he was saying.

'Another couple of days. The boss isn't going to be happy about that. You'd better hope that ship of yours is repaired soon.' The voices began to fade as the three men made their way deeper into the tunnel.

Gemma waited until the light from the torches disappeared and then let out a deep breath.

'You OK,' he asked, dropping down onto the solid floor. He held a hand out to help Gemma from the short drop.

'Fine thanks, although for a minute I thought they might discover our hiding place. So what do we do now? I mean we can't go back towards the folly in case we get discovered.'

'That's true,' said Dan, turning the light back on his phone. 'Let's carry on and see where this leads us.'

'I wonder who those two men were?' asked Gemma.

'I think I know,' said Dan. 'They've been staying at The Ship. Their vessel is out in the bay. They're waiting for engine parts.'

'So, what do you think's going on?'

'Well, they're not starting up a guided tour of a newly found smugglers' cave, that's for sure.'

Gemma picked up the dry tone in his voice and gave a half laugh. 'No, that would be stretching it a bit too far.'

'Whatever they're up to I'm sure it's not legal.'

'But it doesn't answer the main question.'

Dan stopped and turned towards Gemma.

'Yes, what has it got to do with Brian and Penny, and where are they?' she asked.

Dan resumed walking. 'That question has been turning over in my mind as well. As far as I know Brian doesn't know either Tovey or Norton. How about Penny?'

'Never heard her mention either of them and I doubt they would move in the same circles.'

Dan said nothing for a moment. 'Come on, we're nearly there, I'm sure I can hear the sea.'

Gemma could hear the sound of waves breaking on the shore line, and all too soon the passageway began to widen until they could see an opening up ahead.

'Well, look at this,' said Dan as they exited the cave and came onto a tiny cove. 'Do you know where we are?'

Gemma shook her head. She looked above her trying to get her bearings. They were surround by high cliffs. It looked as though there had been a rock fall at one time or another. Larger rocks had fallen into the sea barring entry to the cove apart from a very narrow waterway.

'I think we're further up the coast from the folly,' she said, looking both ways.

Dan began investigating the beach. It wasn't very big. Large boulders surrounded a stretch of sand on both sides. He walked along the sand before spotting something to his left.

'Look, a boat,' he said, walking over to a small motor boat hidden behind one of the boulders. 'So that's how they got here.' He stared out at the horizon seeing the broken shipping vessel in the distance.

Gemma walked towards the boat. There was nothing to identify it.

'Their own little car park,' said Dan, as he walked back to Gemma's side. 'They can come and go as they please without being noticed.'

'I suppose this place could be charted somewhere but it looks pretty concealed to me and I can't remember my dad ever mentioning it.'

A murmur of voices could be heard coming from inside the cave.

'Quick,' said Dan, grabbing her hand. 'They're coming back.'

He pulled her towards a large boulder and they both crouched behind it, hidden from view.

They watched as the two men emerged from the cave and walked over to the boat. They pushed it towards the water and both jumped in. The engine sprang to life and the boat headed out to sea.

Dan stood up. 'Come on, let's get back while the coast is clear. If we're lucky Norton will have left by now so we won't be spotted.'

Gemma followed closely behind. Another piece of the puzzle had been solved. They were definitely getting closer.

12

Luck was on their side and the journey back through the tunnel and out of the folly passed without incident with no sign of Norton.

'So what do we do now? Tell the police?' asked Gemma as they pushed their way through the thick gorse hedge and headed back along the cliff top.

'And tell them what?'

'Tell them what we've found out of course,' said Gemma, irritated at his reaction.

Dan halted and stared down at her, his eyes glinting. 'What have we found out though? A secret door leading to a tunnel. Tovey or Norton could have discovered it and are having a boys own adventure exploring all the passage-ways.'

Gemma clenched her fingers. 'What about the two men?'

Dan shrugged. 'Maybe Norton met them in the pub, got talking and they were interested in seeing the caves. Simple explanation.' He reached out, placed his hands on her shoulders. 'Look Gemma. I know we need to find Brian and Penny. If I thought for one moment the police would act on what we have now I'd be all for going to them and urging them to chase up our findings, but we simply don't have enough evidence.'

Gemma could see that Dan was making sense. She stamped her feet on the ground. 'Oooh, it's so frustrating. Why can't we get a break?'

She felt Dan give her shoulders a gentle shake and she looked at his intense blue eyes. 'We're getting there,' he said. 'Just a few more boxes to tick and I'm sure we'll find them. OK?'

She gave him a half smile. 'OK. So do you have a plan?'

'We need to do a little research. Can we go back to your place and do some checking on the internet? The Wi-fi at

Whitey's is a bit hit and miss to be honest or I'd suggest we go back there.'

'Sure, no problem, but care to tell me what research we will be doing?' she asked as she followed Dan along the path.

'We need to find a connection between Tovey and Bradshaw. I'm sure that's the missing link and I'm almost certain it has to do with the school Norton and Bradshaw went to.'

Gemma thought for a moment. 'Are you thinking maybe the third person expelled along with the other two was Tovey?'

Dan nodded as he reached to take her hand.

'Would you get this information off the internet?' Gemma wasn't sure. She, along with millions of others, used the web, but her use was mainly Facebook or researching the market for her illustrations.

'You'd be amazed what you can find out online,' Dan assured her. 'Come on. Let's do a bit of sleuthing.'

She gave a wry smile. She had to admit even when she felt a bit low, Dan brought a smile to her face.

* * *

The house was empty. Gemma explained that her parents were out for the day. Gone off to pick up a part for the yacht apparently.

Dan had promised Bob and Carol he would take care of their daughter. So far, it'd worked out OK, but he had a feeling it was going to get dangerous anytime soon.

'I'll make coffee. You power up the computer,' said Gemma, leading him into a small room that was used as an office.

'Make mine a large one,' said Dan, settling himself down in front of the screen and putting his glasses on. 'Oh, and if there are any chocolate biscuits going, I wouldn't say no.'

'I'll raid the biscuit tin,' said Gemma over her shoulder as she walked back towards the kitchen.

Waiting for the computer to come to life, Dan could hear Gemma moving about in the kitchen. The rattle of mugs and opening of cupboards and the soft sound of her humming sounded so much like his grandmother as she busied herself looking after him and Brian. He wondered how long it had been since he had thought about his life with his grandmother — a long time, he admitted to himself.

With a deep sigh he returned to the task in hand and within minutes he found the start of the information he was looking for. He looked around the desk and found a pad and pen.

He was soon immersed in the history of Kale College, built in the late 1800s which appeared to have a good reputation for an only boys boarding school, although from what he could tell nobody famous came out of the school, just a long list of professionals. The school upgraded in the 1990s to take girls, day attendance only, after the number of boys going to private school began to reduce.

'Any luck?' said Gemma as she pulled a chair up beside him.

'Just boring stuff so far.' He pushed his notes in front of her to read.

He keyed in the word 'expelled' and was disappointed to find no useful information apart from a few comments about it being a rare occurrence at the school. Dan wasn't sure he quite believed that statement. He could remember quite a few expulsions during his own time at school. Kale College most likely wanted to shy away from anything that would give the school a bad name.

He tried to find a list of pupils' names but only came across past and present teachers. It was disappointing as he'd hoped it would lead him to Tovey's name. He did, however, find a link to a Facebook page for 'Friends of Kale College', a site for ex-pupils. He clicked on the link and was further frustrated to find that it was a closed group. Another dead end.

He paused for a moment and picked up his mug. He breathed in the rich aroma before taking an appreciating swallow, the strength of the coffee hitting his taste buds. He picked up a biscuit from the plate and popped it, whole, into his mouth, the combination of rich coffee and sweet chocolate making him sigh with pleasure.

He heard Gemma sigh beside him.

'You OK?'

She stretched her arms above her head and tried to divert a yawn from escaping. 'Sorry, I'd hoped we'd find something quicker than this.'

'Most research is tedious and time consuming. We could be doing this for some time.'

She pushed her chair back and stood up. 'I think I'll leave you to it.'

He watched her pick up a sketch book and settle down in a comfy chair.

'Helps me relax,' she said, opening the pad.

He watched her for a moment. The

pencil in her hand moving swiftly across the page.

He returned to the screen, deciding to apply for membership of the closed group stating that he'd been a pupil at the school years ago and was trying to catch up with a view to a meet up with old class mates. He tried to think of a name that would not appear unusual but not too ordinary, deciding that John Taylor sounded just about right. Realising he didn't know what years Norton and Bradshaw attended the school he guessed the early seventies so put in the first five years of that decade and crossed his fingers that it would be about right and he'd get access soon.

He searched for another five minutes for any further information about Kale College but found nothing he didn't already know.

Wondering what to do next he tapped in Hugo Tovey and pressed search. He knew he'd owned his own business which failed, but knew little else. It may be worth investigating.

Tovey Investments operated for about 20 years, in and around the London area, mainly dealing in property, buying up houses, selling some for large profits, others he rented out. By the look of it he wasn't a good landlord. The list of complaints against him were long. Shoddy or little repairs done and high rents. He was made bankrupt about five years ago. A very nasty court case. A tenant was left in a wheelchair after falling through a rotted staircase. So where did he get the money to buy Westlea Manor?

He moved that thought to one side as he heard a ping of an incoming message from Facebook. He'd been accepted into the private group. It seemed quite easy after that. He introduced himself and stated his intentions of meeting up with old friends after being out of the country for a number of years. He pushed it a little further by saying he was in the same class as Norton Bradshaw and remembered they got in a bit of trouble but he'd left before he knew what happened to them. He had no idea if either man kept up on Facebook, but doubted it.

He sat back, stretched his arms above his head and waited to see if he received any reply.

He didn't have to wait long. Within a couple of minutes a chap called Michael answered. He thought he remembered John but knew Norton and Bradshaw much better. He seemed to want to chat so Dan asked a couple of vague questions about school life and what was Michael doing now before getting to the question he really wanted answered. Who was the third boy?

He watched the screen, waiting for Michael to tell him it was Tovey. How disappointed he was when a name he'd never heard of came on the screen — Stephen Henderson. Who on earth was he? Michael admitted he thought it was strange that this boy was involved in anything dodgy. He was too quiet according to Michael. One of those boys who stood on the side lines

watching everything but never partici-
pating.

Dan wondered what happened to
Stephen Henderson. Michael must
have read his mind because he continued to reveal more information. It
turned out that after being expelled
Henderson had gone to another private
school in the south of England and
done exceedingly well for himself. He'd
been good at finance and was now a
successful market investor. After a few
more moments of chatting Dan signed
out of the chat room. He took off his
glasses and rubbed tired eyes before
putting them back on.

Gemma was no longer in the office
but he could hear her moving about in
the kitchen. He knew she was going to
be disappointed about Tovey not being
the third boy.

He pushed his glasses back on and
tapped the name Stephen Henderson
into the search engine. A business
website site popped up and Dan hit
the 'about me' button. Surprisingly,

Stephen hadn't been born with a silver spoon in his mouth. He'd won a bursary to go to Kale College. There was a mention of the school and how after a small indiscretion he was expelled. Surprisingly honest of him, observed Dan, most people wouldn't advertise past mistakes. After losing the bursary, his parents both worked at two jobs to pay for more private education.

Dan scanned through the rest of the history. Henderson certainly repaid his parents. There was a picture of them relaxing at their retirement home in Spain which their son had paid for, along with a picture of the man himself sitting at a desk, a serious look on his face as he stared into the camera. Maybe he was mixed up with Tovey? Maybe he put up the money to buy the Manor?

'How's it going?'

Dan pulled himself away from the screen and looked up. Gemma stood in the doorway, a couple of mugs of coffee in her hand.

'It wasn't Tovey,' he said, deciding to come straight out with it. He saw the disappointment on Gemma's face and wanted to reach out a give her a comforting hug. Instead he repeated what information he'd discovered and watched as Gemma's shoulders began to slump.

'So where do we go from here?' she said, handing him one of the mugs before sitting back down in the corner chair.

Dan pulled off his glasses and rubbed a hand over his chin. 'I think we should go and see this Stephen Henderson. He lives about an hour's drive from here.'

Gemma raised an eyebrow. 'Why? What help would that be?'

'I'm not sure. It might be a wild goose chase but I just have a feeling that he might be able to help us.'

She gave him another puzzled look. 'So how is meeting this Henderson chap going to help us find Brian and Penny?'

He took a sip from his coffee before

answering. 'I think he holds information which could help us. It's just a hunch on my part.'

He watched Gemma turning over his words in her head. Hunches were what he was quite good at. Often on his travels he'd get a feeling that there would be hidden gems that people would be interested in. He'd spend a considerable amount of time finding an off the beaten track beauty spot or a monument with history. Yes, his hunches more often than not paid off.

'OK, I'll go with your hunch, but how are you going to get Stephen Henderson to talk? I mean, do you think it's a good idea just to turn up and ask him outright?'

Dan frowned. He had to agree she had a point.

'I'll ring him first.'

'And say what? 'Hello Mr Henderson, my name is Dan Jackson and I believe that you know a man named Tovey who I think knows what has happened to my brother and his girlfriend who have disappeared.''

Even to Dan's ears it sounded unbelievable and he could just imagine that Henderson would shut the door in his face if he turned up with that tale. There must be another way. He thought for a moment until a plan came into his head.

'I'm going to give him a ring, say I'm a writer, doing an article on men making good after being expelled from school.'

'I'm sure he'd love to be reminded of that,' huffed Gemma.

'You'd be surprised. Men like to boast about how well they've done. Leave it with me.' He tried to sound more confident than he was and privately crossed his fingers.

Gemma shrugged. 'OK. I'll leave you to it. Fancy a sandwich?'

Dan suddenly realised he'd not eaten since breakfast. 'That would be great, thanks.'

Gemma nodded and left him to his phone call. He was surprised when five minutes later he'd spoken to Stephen Henderson who said he would be delighted to talk about his 'bad boy made good' episode as he called it and Dan arranged the visit for the next day.

'How did it go?' asked Gemma, walking into the room with a plate of ham and cheese sandwiches in her hand.

'Do you think we can borrow your dad's car again tomorrow?'

'He agreed?'

'He agreed,' confirmed Dan, reaching out for a sandwich and taking a healthy bite. Food never tasted so good.

* * *

Wanting to stretch their legs, Dan and Gemma decided on a walk along the seafront. It was late afternoon. The sun managed to work itself out from behind the grey clouds, even the sea showed signs of a blue tinge.

'Do you really think that we'll find our answers tomorrow?' asked Gemma, as they stopped to watch a surfer catch the last of the waves.

'If not all our answers I'm sure we'll get a step further,' Dan replied.

Gemma heaved a huge sigh. 'I sometimes wonder whether this nightmare we're in will ever end and if we'll find Brian and Penny.'

Dan pulled her closer to his side. 'It will end, I promise, and we'll find them. Have no doubt about that.'

Gemma gave him a watery smile, clinging to his words of reassurance.

'I really must get back to work,' she said after a moment. She told him about the author who'd authorised her to do a run of pictures for a children's book she was writing.

'It's new territory for me,' she explained, confessing she was worried she wouldn't come up to the writer's expectations.

'I'm sure you'll do great,' said Dan. 'Just looking at the work you've done while I've been in your company shows me what a talent you have.'

Gemma laughed and gave him a sharp nudge in the ribs. 'You flatter me.'

'No flattery intended. I'm absolutely serious.'

'Thanks,' she said. 'You know you're lucky. Apart from my parents you're the only one I've ever shared my illustrations with. Well, the early stages of them that is. Of course others have seen them when they buy the cards.' She stopped speaking suddenly and put a hand to her mouth. 'Sorry, I'm babbling. Seem to do that all the time when I'm talking about my work.'

'Babble away, I like it. But I know what you mean. I'm much the same. Very rarely share my work. Brian's not really interested unless it's some sunny beach where he can lie and catch the rays.'

'Ah, no wonder he and Penny have so much in common. She likes nothing better than to soak up the sun and improve her tan.'

'And you, Gemma. What do you like to do?'

'That's easy. Explore. There's nothing more satisfying than finding hidden gems when you are in a new place. There's always something that comes as a surprise.'

'A girl after my own heart,' said Dan and realised that he meant it.

They reached a parade of shops and Gemma stopped. 'I used the last of the bread,' she said. 'Better get some before Mum comes home.'

'I'll wait here,' said Dan.

'Won't be a moment.'

He watched her disappear inside a small supermarket before wandering along the shop parade. Right at the end stood a travel agent's and he looked at the window display to see what was on offer. He was pleased to see a trip to China was posted on one big display. It had been well worth his recent trip and he knew that his article would go down well with those travellers who were looking for something different.

He went to turn away when the door opened and Whitey stepped out.

'Oh, sorry dearie. Didn't see you there,' she said, quickly tucking the brochure she held in her hand into an over-large handbag.

'Booking your holiday?' asked Dan, nodding towards the brochure sticking out of her bag.

'Oh, no. One of the guests asked me to get some brochures for him,' she said, pushing them further into her bag and pulling the zip closed.

'Hi Whitey,' said Gemma coming up behind them, a carrier bag in her hand.

'I was just asking if Whitey was going on holiday,' said Dan. When Gemma gave him a questioning glance he added, 'I bumped into her as she was coming out of the travel agent.'

'Whitey, go on holiday? Never known her to, although I think she deserves a break after all these years looking after others.'

'No time for holidays. Anyway I'm happy staying in Westlea looking after all my guests. I thought you promised to come and see me while you were back home,' she said, wagging a finger at Gemma. 'Apart from a swift hello the other day I've not seen you.'

'Sorry, been a bit busy showing this man here the area.'

Whitey patted her on the shoulders. 'OK, I'll forgive you this time but don't forget to call in for a natter before you go back to the big city.'

'Will do, I promise.'

'Well, must be getting on,' said Whitey. With a brief wave off she went.

Dan watched her walked along the pavement. Strange that she was getting a brochure for a guest. He was sure the last guest apart from himself booked out this morning. Oh well, he'd been out all day, maybe a new guest had arrived in his absence. He tossed away the thought, replacing it with important ones.

13

The chocolate box cottage was a surprise to Dan. After reading up on Stephen Henderson he'd expected something a little more opulent than what he saw before him. A lavender flanked path leading to a porch with a climbing rose hugging the frame. A thatched roof completed the picture.

'Nice, but not my cup of tea,' said Gemma, as she stepped out of the car.

He was surprised, thinking that this was the type of property she would go for.

Gemma must have picked up on something from his look.

'Oh, don't get me wrong, it's OK but I'm more for the modern look.' She opened the gate. 'Come on, let's see what Henderson has to say for himself.'

Stephen Henderson was about 15 years older than the picture on the internet. His hair was thinner on top and the years hadn't been kind. Small in stature, with a rotund waistline, Dan couldn't see him getting into any kind of trouble.

They were led into a lounge with two large comfy sofas, accompanied with traditional dark wood furniture and the obligatory inglenook fireplace with a wood burner set in the middle giving off a healthy glow.

They settled themselves down and a woman who was introduced as Margaret, his wife, brought in a tray of coffee before excusing herself explaining that she was in the middle of canning some fruit for the winter.

'So what can I do to help you?' said Henderson, his voice mild like the man himself.

'As I said on the phone I'm researching a book on men made good after being expelled from school,' said Dan, pulling out a notebook and pen out of his pocket.

Henderson looked at him for a

moment before steepling his fingers under his chin and giving Dan an assessing look.

He must have liked what he saw as he dropped his hands to his side and leant back into the sofa.

'So tell me. How did you find out about me being expelled from school?'

Dan expected the question and while they were driving discussed it with Gemma who agreed on the course of action they would take.

'Gemma knows someone who was at school with you. He got drunk one night at a party and told the story of how he was expelled along with a couple of other boys. He mentioned your name. To be honest when she told me the story that's where I got the idea for the article. So I checked out your name on the internet although I wasn't expecting to find anything but came across your website. I was surprised to see how much you'd accomplished. You even mention your expulsion from school.

To be honest, I was even more intrigued.'

Henderson didn't ask who the person was, just gave Dan another long look.

'I must confess, after receiving your phone call I checked you out. You've written some interesting articles. So this will be a departure for you?' Henderson said, after a moment.

'Hopefully a good one,' said Dan.

'Indeed. So, tell me, which one of my accomplices is known to you?'

Gemma looked up from her inspection of the flower design on her coffee cup. 'Alan Bradshaw.'

'Ah, another follower,' said Henderson, giving a wry smile.

'Follower?' asked Dan, frowning.

Henderson put his cup on the coffee table and tapped his fingers along the arm of the sofa, a faraway look taking over his features before he came back to the present.

'Have you ever been bullied?' he asked Dan.

'Bullied? Well no, not that I can remember.'

'Oh, you'd remember if it happened to you,' Henderson assured him.

'In the era I went to school in seemed to happen a lot. You'd have the main bully boy, then his followers, and then the poor devil who was the brunt of it. I was the brunt.'

He paused for a moment and Dan saw a flash of pain cross his eyes as Henderson remembered his school days.

'You know, my parents were just ordinary working class people who happened to have a son who excelled at maths. They were so proud when I won a bursary to Kale College. They both worked overtime at their jobs to pay for the expensive uniform and other accessories I needed. The day they took me to the school for my first day, they wore their Sunday best, even though they looked out of place among the designer clothes worn by the other parents.'

Dan smiled imagining the scene.

'I was frightened,' continued Henderson, 'but excited all the same. Bradshaw and Norton — he was my other accomplice — befriended me straight away. They arrived at the school a term before me so were settled into the routine. I was flattered that they wanted to be my friends.'

Dan listened as Henderson's tale unfolded. How slowly Bradshaw and Norton pulled him into their circle and then slowly began to turn on him. Stealing his pocket money, forcing him to carry out pranks that became more dangerous as time went by. Dan could only feel for the poor child whose only wish was to gain as much as possible from a private education.

'I tried to get away from them but bullies never let go. Once they have a victim they seem to gain in strength. In the end I was terrified every time they approached me, wondering what they would come up with next to mentally torture me.'

'Couldn't you go to your teachers or even your parents?' asked Gemma, entering the conversation for the first time.

Henderson spread his hands apart. 'It was an all-boys school. I'm sure the teachers were fully aware of what was going on but as long as no one got hurt they tended to ignore the problem. Thank goodness those days are long gone. As for my parents — how could I? They wanted me to do well. I was going places. I would put up with anything not to let them down. Although, of course, in the end, it didn't work out that way. By the way, what is Bradshaw doing now?'

Dan and Gemma both looked at him in surprise at the change of subject.

'Oh, he's a pharmacist. Owns a chemist shop in my home town,' said Gemma.

'Ah, no surprise there. He always did seem to have a way with chemicals, although I must admit he did have other talents.'

'Really. What were they?' asked Gemma.

'Seemed he was quite a talent at gardening.'

'Sorry, you've lost me,' said Dan, leaning forward in his seat.

'He and Norton used to spend quite a bit of time in an old shed on the far side of the rugby field, hidden away from sight by a cluster of trees. Nobody ever went there, at least, none of the teachers. Well, not until they got caught.'

'Got caught?' Dan frowned. What on earth was Henderson on about?

'They'd been bragging about how well their plants were growing in the shed.'

'No harm in that, surely?' said Gemma.

Henderson gave her a long look. 'Let's put it like this. They weren't growing tomatoes.'

'Ahh,' said Dan, suddenly realising what Henderson was on about.

'So, how did you become involved in it?' enquired Dan.

Henderson shrugged. 'Like any school boy, I was curious and one day they invited me, and I say that very loosely, to visit their shed. I should have known when they pulled me along that I shouldn't be going but they told me that if I followed them the bullying would stop.' Henderson paused for a moment and a smile tugged his lips. 'What a fool I was.'

'So what happened?'

'By some stroke of misfortune we were in the shed looking at 'the plants' and, to be honest, I didn't know what they were when a teacher who'd heard the gossip about plants being grown decided to investigate and, as they say, the game was up.'

'So you were all expelled?'

Henderson nodded. 'Although the real ring leader got away clean and was never caught.'

He must have seen the look of surprised on Dan's face and continued.

'As I've already explained Bradshaw was a follower as was Norton but there's always a leader, the one that comes up with the ideas although maybe not the brains. There was an older boy, the ring leader of the group. He was the worst bully of all. He must have known that something was going to happened. Don't ask me how he knew but he was nowhere near the shed when the teacher discovered the little enterprise they had going.'

He paused for a moment and reached for his coffee. 'I left that school in disgrace. My parents, I shall never forget the look on their faces the day they collected me. I vowed that I would never let them down again. It wasn't long before I confessed that I was nothing to do with the episode but by then it was too late. I couldn't go back, not that I wanted to. Anyway, I managed to get into the local grammar school, studied hard, went on to university and became what I am today. On the quiet I work with a local volunteer group to stamp out bullying in all walks of life.' He put down his coffee and looked straight at Dan. 'And that's it. My life story.'

'You've done well,' said Dan, looking around the room.

'Thank you. To be honest I've worked long hours to achieve where I am today. I don't regret what happened to me. I suppose you can say that it made me the man I am now.' He grinned. 'Let's just say you learn from your mistakes.'

He stood up and looked at his watch. 'Well, I think you must have all the information you need. I've promised my wife lunch out today and it's getting to that time now.' He scratch his head, a frown creasing his brow. 'Can I ask that you don't mention Bradshaw or Norton if you write about me? I know it's on public record, but unless they agree I wouldn't be happy with their names appearing.'

'No problem,' Dan assured him. 'The article will be focused only on you. Can I ask you one last question — who was the other boy?'

'Oh sorry, didn't I say. Tovey. Hugo Tovey.'

Dan looked at Gemma and saw the surprise on her face. Henderson must have noticed it too.

'You know the name?'

Gemma nodded. 'He's just moved into my home town. Bought a large manor house and is planning to turn it into a conference centre.'

Henderson scoffed at the snippet of information. 'I'm surprised he's got the brains. If Tovey and Bradshaw are in the same town I wouldn't be surprised if Norton isn't far behind. They were a close knit group. All I can say is watch out. They could be up to something.'

'Surely people change over the years?' Gemma replied.

'Most do, and perhaps I'm being a bit ungracious. I don't think so, though.'

The door opened and his wife walked in and tapped her watch.

'Be with you in a minute, dear,' he said, giving his wife a smile.

'Well, thank you for all your help,' said Dan shaking his hand, 'and sorry for taking up so much of your time.

'No problem and good luck with your article,' he said, showing them out.

★   ★   ★

'What do you make of all that?' said Gemma as they headed back towards Westlea Bay.

'Well, we've found the connection. Didn't I tell you that Henderson was going to be full of information?'

'At last we seem to be getting somewhere. So what next?'

'Lunch. I'm starving.'

Gemma looked at him in surprise. 'Shouldn't we tell the police? I mean, we've found the connection. Surely they will have to investigate Tovey now.'

'I still don't think it's enough and it still doesn't tell us what happened to Brian and Penny.'

'What do you mean 'what happened'?' Gemma's face turned white and she felt sick. 'You don't think they're . . . '

Dan stopped her before she went any further. 'Sorry, I didn't mean to alarm you. No, I don't think anything dreadful has happened to them. I think they are fine. Look, I'll ring the police, tell them what we've found out, see what they say.'

'OK,' said Gemma, releasing the breath she didn't know she was holding.

'Come on, let's head back home. We can have lunch at The Ship if you like. Whitey informed me this morning that fresh sea bass was on the menu today.'

'Sounds delicious.'

'Great, and you can catch up with Whitey while I'm making the call to the police.'

'Sounds good to me,' said Gemma, feeling more assured now that the authorities would be informed. She wasn't sure why Dan seemed a little hesitant. She was convinced they were close to finding the missing couple and revealing what sort of criminal activity that the three men were involved in. She hoped that at last the terrible nightmare was finally going to be over. Little did she know that in the next 48 hours things were going to get even worse.

14

The Ship was full of diners when they arrived. Whitey look harassed as she bumped into them on her way to the kitchen.

'Hello dearies. Sorry, can't stop and chat. A group of ramblers decided they wanted to stop off for lunch before taking a walk along the coastal path to the next town. Chef's up to his eyes in orders. One of the waiters decided not to turn up today so I've stepped in to help.'

'Don't suppose you have a spare table for us?' asked Gemma, peering into the dining room.

'There's one in the far corner,' said Whitey, 'although you'll have to wait a while for lunch.'

'That's fine,' Gemma assured her. 'Dan tells me you have sea bass on the menu. Hope it's still available.'

'For two?' asked Whitey, pulling out a pad from among her flowing skirts and jotting down the order as Gemma nodded.

Whitey disappeared into the kitchen leaving Dan and Gemma to find their table.

'I'll go and get us a drink,' said Dan. 'Wine?'

'A small glass of white, please.'

She watched him walk away, pulling his phone out of his pocket as he headed towards the bar. She just hoped that Dan would convince the police to act on the information they'd collated but she had an uneasy feeling that it wasn't going to be the case. She turned her attention back to the dining room. Dodging numerous backpacks lying by the side of tables she made her way across the room and settled into her seat.

There was a buzz of chatter surrounding her and she leant back in her chair thinking over what Henderson had revealed. Bullying and growing illegal substances — it was all a different world from her own.

'Penny for them,' said Dan as he placed a glass of wine in front of her before settling in his own seat.

'Sorry,' she said, wrapping her hands around the wine glass before taking a sip. 'I was just thinking about that poor man and the bullying. What an awful thing to happen to him.'

'I was thinking the same thing. You know, although I'm not a journalist as such, it would make a good article.'

'So you think you could write something about it? I mean, I know we went to visit Mr Henderson with the story that you were going to write an article and it's not strictly the truth, but maybe you should.'

'I was thinking the same thing,' said Dan, picking up his pint. 'Not me personally. I just don't think I could get the message across but I know someone who might be interested. I'll give him a call and see what he thinks about it.'

'Did you ring the police?' said Gemma.

Dan nodded. 'I told them what we'd found out but they're still not sure that Brian and Penny are even missing. They still haven't found the car and from what they said they still think they've gone off somewhere for some private time.'

'Private time? What a load of nonsense.'

Dan reached over the table and squeezed her hand. 'We'll find them, Gemma. With or without the police.'

Gemma felt the warmth of Dan's fingers. 'Thanks, I needed just a little reassurance.'

'Glad I could be of help,' he said, his eyes locking onto her own.

The sound of a chair scraping against the floor pulled Gemma away from Dan's gaze but not before she noted the smile that played on his lips. Sometimes he made it impossible for her to concentrate on the matter in hand. She shivered and pulled her hand out of his grasp.

'Looks as though the place is

clearing,' said Dan, nodding towards the ramblers who were gathering their belongings and heading out.

They didn't have to wait long, a few moments later Whitey appeared carrying two large plates filled with fish and steaming vegetables.

'Enjoy,' she said, before she began moving among the tables collecting the debris left by the ramblers.

Gemma squeezed the slice of lemon over her sea bass and cut into the flesh. 'Delicious,' she said, closing her eyes and letting her taste buds take in the different flavours.

Dan laughed and tucked into his own food, nodding his appreciation.

'Why does it always taste so much better when you're near the sea?'

'Because it's caught daily and served fresh. None of your frozen fish here. Just the taste of the sea,' replied Gemma.

'Well, I for one, appreciate it all the more. What more can any man ask for. Wonderful food, a pint of beer and a beautiful woman.' He reached for his glass and raised it in a salute.

Gemma noted the twinkle in his eye. 'Flatterer,' she said, 'although I'm not sure I should be included in the same sentence as a pint of beer and a piece of fish.'

She watched as he placed a hand over his heart. 'I'm wounded that you don't take my words as a compliment,' he said, before winking at her and making Gemma laugh even more.

He was, of course, trying to take her mind of her worries. That's what she was beginning to like about him. The way he would try to ease any of her concerns without her even noticing.

'So where do we go from here? I mean, we've found the connection between Tovey, Norton and Bradshaw which leads us to a connection with Brian and Penny. Should we confront Tovey? Tell him what we've found out?'

Dan popped the last piece of fish in his mouth.

'I doubt that would help,' he said, putting his knife and fork down and pushing his plate away. 'I mean, he'd just laugh in your face, plus it could be dangerous taking that path.'

'I suppose you're right,' said Gemma, her shoulders drooping in defeat. 'So have you any better ideas.'

Dan rubbed a hand across his chin and looked thoughtful. 'Well, I do have one thought.'

'Oh yes, and what's that?'

'Follow the money.'

'Follow what money?' asked Gemma, wondering what he was talking about.

'Well, I've been thinking. Where did Tovey get the money to buy Westlea Manor? According to all the information we've managed to find out about him he lost it all a few years ago. So where did he get the cash to buy a place like the manor?'

'Squirrelled some away,' suggested Gemma. 'Offshore account? A loan from the bank?'

'Could be, but I'm not so sure.

Remember what Henderson said about him not having much of a brain?'

'Well he must have had something going for him to run a successful business.'

'Mm, could be, but I think he was successful because of his bullying, not because of his business sense. No, I'm almost certain there is someone else in the mix. Someone that we don't know about yet . . . '

Gemma shuddered. The thought of someone else being involved didn't sound good and she hoped that Dan was wrong, but before she could voice her concerns Whitey approached them.

'Thank goodness that's over. My feet are killing me,' she said, dropping into a chair and giving a deep sigh. 'Of course, I'm glad of the custom. As you know the winter months are long and hard for those of us who depend on the summer months to see us through the storms of the other six months of the year.'

'Oh dear, Whitey,' said Gemma, a

genuine look of concern crossing her features. 'Maybe it's time to pack it all up and retire.'

Whitey shook her head. 'Not me, dearie. Here until they pack me off in a box.'

'Whitey, I'm sure you still have a good many years at The Ship.'

'Not if I'm rushed off my feet like today,' remarked Whitey, giving out a laugh and changing the subject. 'Anyway, how was the sea bass?'

'Cooked to perfection. My compliments to the chef,' said Gemma.

'I'll tell him. It'll make his day. Likes a compliment or two. Not many, mind, or he'll be asking for a big pay rise.' She adjusted her flowing skirts and pulled off the brightly coloured scarf that she used as a bandana around her head and pushed back a stray lock of hair from falling into her line of vision. The bracelets around her wrists jangled along with the bell necklace she always wore.

'Anyway, how are you Gemma? I

thought you promised to come and see me while you're visiting your parents. I've hardly seen you.'

'I know, I'm sorry, Whitey. Time seems to have flown by and Dan wanted to visit so many places.'

'Hey, don't blame me,' said Dan, 'you are the one that offered.'

Gemma grinned and reached out and patted his hand. 'So I did.'

'Seems to me that it wasn't such a hardship,' observed Whitey. 'So how is London? Still enjoying the big city?'

'Well, it took a little adjusting to but I think it was a good move. I've acclimatised myself to the metropolitan lifestyle. I've made a few friends but my business keeps me pretty busy.'

'That's good. I suppose you'll miss your mum and dad when they go on their travels?'

Gemma looked at her in surprise. How on earth did Whitey know about that? From what she understood from her mother, neither of her parents had mentioned it to anyone other than herself? Perhaps it wasn't such a big secret.

'I met your mother in town yesterday and she was telling me about the trip they're planning.'

'They're going to have a wonderful time and maybe I'll go and meet up with them from time to time. That campervan is big enough to fit a large family in.'

'Sounds like a wonderful adventure,' said Whitey, impressed.

'You should take a trip yourself,' said Gemma, picking up the wistful note in the woman's voice.

'One day, maybe. Anyway, back to you. Hasn't that friend of yours, Penny, joined you in London?'

'Yes, but I haven't met up with her yet. Think she's too busy with her boyfriend and settling into her new job. I'll ring her when I get back and arrange to meet up.'

'You do that, dearie. Friends are important. Doesn't do to lose touch with people. I wish in my life I'd kept in touch with people . . . '

'Anyone in particular?' asked Gemma, wondering if Whitey ever had someone special in her life apart from her husband.

Whitey shook her head. 'No, just a few guests that could have turned out to be good friends if I'd have put in a bit more effort. Anyway, don't forget to get in touch with Penny. Good friendships are hard to come by.'

Whitey stood up. 'Well things to do. Must get on.' She patted Gemma on the shoulders and, with her skirts rustling around her, she headed back towards the kitchen.

'News travels fast,' said Dan watching Whitey walk into the kitchen and close the door.

Gemma shrugged. 'The Ship can be a place of gossip. I mean, how would you have learnt about Bradshaw and Norton if you hadn't picked up the information over a game of dominoes?'

'True, but didn't you find it odd that she wanted to know about Penny?'

'Yeah, that was a bit strange. I didn't know she knew Penny that well. I'm almost sure that it isn't Sam Tremayne's local, think he drinks in The Seagull's Nest which is further along the bay.'

She was about to say more when her mobile bleeped. 'Have to go. Dad wants the car back,' she said, draining the last of her wine and pushing back her chair. 'We still haven't decided where we go from here.'

Dan rose from his seat. 'First I'm going to contact my mate about the bullying article and then I need to check on this money business. It's still bugging me to be honest . . . '

Gemma got the sense he was being evasive but decided to leave it. She was sure Dan would squirrel out any information that he could find. After he promised to contact her as soon as he had any information, she said goodbye.

★ ★ ★

252

Dan watched until Gemma was out of sight and then headed to his room. He turned on his laptop. While he waited for the connection to go through he made himself a coffee from the facilities provided.

He'd missed something. He'd felt it the night he saw Bradshaw outside the pub and again today. He just couldn't put his finger on whatever it was. He poured boiling water onto the coffee granules and added a generous amount of sugar hoping the rush would get his brain moving in the right direction. He breathed in the aroma of the coffee and took a sip before settling down at his laptop and began to search through the mire of information on Hugo Tovey and his business affairs. There must be a clue somewhere.

Four hours later and he was still no further forward. There was nothing he could find about Tovey's business that showed that he could have hidden any money.

Dan pulled off his glasses and

scrubbed a hand over tired eyes. He stood up and stretched. He'd go through it again and again until he found what he was looking for. He made another cup of coffee and sat back down at the laptop. Perhaps going another route might tell him the answers he needed.

Another hour and he sat back, a smile on his face. He'd found another link. He just needed a little more information.

He reached for his mobile and dialled.

'It's me. I'm coming up to London in the morning. Need to check on something then I think we'll have all the information to move ahead. Gemma's still in the dark and I'd like to keep it that way. She'll be safer not knowing anything. To be honest I'd like to carry on without her from now on but I don't think it's possible.' He smiled to himself as he thought of how feisty Gemma could be. 'She wants to find her friend and nothing is going to stop her. She's going to be safer with me by her side. I'll ring you in the morning and we can meet up before I head back here.'

He listened for a few more minutes before saying goodbye.

Hang on in there, Brian, he said to himself as he readied himself for bed. *Hopefully by the end of tomorrow I'll have found you and sorted this whole mess out.*

15

'Honestly, men!' exclaimed Gemma the next morning as she walked into the kitchen.

Her mother looked up from her crossword puzzle. 'Oh dear. What's put you in a bad mood this morning?'

'Dan,' said Gemma, reaching into the bread bin and pulling out two slices of bread.

Carol looked down at her puzzle. 'Lover's tiff?'

'Mother, really. We're just friends.'

'No. I meant the clue in my crossword.' Carol tapped the paper with her pen.

'Oh right, sorry.' She popped the bread into the toaster and reached for the kettle. 'How many letters?'

'Four.'

Gemma filled the kettle and thought for a moment. 'Spat.'

Carol drew her pen across the spaces. 'Perfect, thanks. So what's Dan done that's got you so upset this morning?'

Gemma busied herself making her breakfast before answering. She needed to cool down after reading Dan's text. She'd told him from the start that they were in this together and then what does he do? Tells her he's off to London first thing this morning to check something out and will be back, hopefully, this afternoon. She rang him immediately but his phone was switched off.

She slapped a generous amount of butter onto her toast and took a large bite, chewing vigorously as she tried to cool her temper.

'Sit down before you explode,' said Carol in a calming voice after Gemma related the text.

Gemma put her breakfast plate in the dishwasher and picked up her mug of tea.

'Honestly, Mum. Don't you think I have a right to be angry?' she said, sitting down opposite her mother and puffing out a deep sigh. She cupped her mug of tea, her knuckles white with anger.

Carol studied her daughter for a moment before saying anything. 'I think you should wait and see what he has to say before you get mad at him. You said he caught the early train to London. Perhaps he didn't want to wake you. You're not the best early riser, are you?'

Gemma took a sip of her tea, the whites of her knuckles evaporating as she acknowledged the truth in her mother's words. 'Well, I suppose he could have thought that.' She remembered the first morning in London when she'd woken late. Dan was up before her, even though he'd just arrived back from China. OK, he'd put it down to jet lag but she got the feeling that he was an early riser anyway.

'I'm sure he'll be back this afternoon with whatever information he's found. Now drink your tea and tell me how your investigation is going.' Carol dropped her pen on the table and leant back in her chair.

Gemma put her hand to her mouth. 'Oh goodness, I haven't told you, have I?'

'Told me what?'

'About the folly. Dan and I went to investigate and guess what we found? A secret passage leading to a small cove that I didn't know existed.' She decided not to mention that they were nearly caught when Norton appeared. That was a little bit too much information for her mother to know. She'd only worry and Gemma didn't want that.

'How exciting. I wonder if the first owner discovered it and built the folly around it?'

'That's what I thought, but I was surprised to find it. I thought all coves and smugglers passages situated around here were documented.'

'So did I. You should check with your dad. He's down at the boat yard. Did I tell you that he's nearly finished the refurbishment? Think it will be ready for a test run and he's talking about taking me away for the weekend.' She chuckled. 'Says I need some practice in the kitchen.'

'Cheeky thing.' Gemma laughed. 'You could produce a three course meal over an open fire if you put your mind to it.'

'I'm not sure about that, but I'm sure I can manage what facilities a camper-van has to offer.'

Gemma turned her thoughts back to documents and smuggling.

'I wonder if I could find any information about Westlea Manor and smuggling. There must be some information somewhere.'

'Take a look on the bookcase. I'm almost sure I've seen a book about the history of Westlea Bay on one of the shelves. Think your father bought it at a book sale a few years ago.' She picked up her pen. 'You know, I must sort out that bookcase. The books your father buys and never reads is getting ridiculous,' she muttered to herself as she went back to her crossword.

'I'll go and check then,' said Gemma. The only response from her mother was a raised hand.

She poured herself another coffee and went to check the contents of her father's bookcase. Her mother was right. The shelves were packed solid with all sorts of books. Her father was an avid reader and liked all kinds of literature from thrillers to biographies, old or new. Gemma ran her fingers along the titles. The books weren't in any sort of order but mixed together, hardbacks leaning against paperbacks. Some were even upside down. Eventually she found it on the bottom shelf. A brown coloured, hardback book, the title, *Westlea Bay — A History*, in gold lettering displayed on the spine. The book was thick with yellowed, liver spotted pages.

Settling herself down, she opened the book. The smell of history hit her from the dusty pages. Checking out the index she went to the chapter on Westlea Manor. The information the writer had gathered was quite in depth and she was surprised to learn that prior to the Manor being built, the land had been used for farming. There were rumours that it was also used for smuggling in the 18th century, particularly in the movement of brandy from France. Gemma was frustrated that there was no mention of a hidden cove or secret passages, but still, even the suggestion of smuggling spiked her interest.

She closed the book, rested her hand on her chin and pondered over what she had discovered. There was still no news from Dan. She looked down at her phone which rested on the arm of her chair, willing it to ring.

Once again anger built up inside her, then she pushed the feeling away. It was useless wasting time on something that she could do nothing about, but he would certainly feel the brunt of her anger when he returned.

She was wondering what to do with herself while she waited for Dan when her mother entered the room.

'Your father's been on the phone. Says he wants us to join him at the boat yard. He has something he wants to show us.'

Gemma raised an enquiring eyebrow.

'Your guess is as good as mine,' said her mother, turning towards the hallway. She took both their jackets off the coat hooks, passing Gemma's leather jacket to her. 'Any luck with the book?' she enquired, slinging her handbag over her shoulder.

'Lots of information,' said Gemma, following her mother out the front door. 'Did you know in the 18th century there was a lot of brandy smuggling going on around here?'

Carol nodded. 'If I remember rightly from my school history lessons it was a common practice to ferry it onto shore to avoid the revenue man. Small ships that could easily manoeuvre around the coves and outrun the authorities.

Smugglers would find caves to hide the contraband until it was safe to move. Finding passages in the caves was a bonus, especially if they burrowed inland a mile or two.'

Gemma shuddered, thinking about the danger of the escapade. She was sure being caught had severe consequences for those who participated. Being sent to the colonies being a favourite action taken by the authorities of the time.

'I wonder what your father is up to?' said Carol as she reversed the car out of the drive and headed toward the boat yard. She gave Gemma a suspicious look.

Gemma shrugged. 'Hey, don't look at me, he's not said a word.'

'Mmm. Bet he's got a surprise for me up his sleeve and he knows how I hate not knowing what's going on.'

Gemma turned to her mother, laughter in her eyes. 'Stop kidding me. You know you like surprises as much as the next person.'

'Anyway we'll soon find out,' admitted Carol.

Carol parked the car, turned off the engine and tapped her fingers on the steering wheel.

'Come on, Mum,' said Gemma, stepping out of the car. If she was honest with herself she couldn't wait to see what was in store for them and wished her father had confided in her on what he was up to.

Bob was waiting outside the boat shed, a wide smile on his face.

'So what's going on?' said Gemma.

'That's what I want to know,' said Carol walking around the car and standing by her daughter.

Bob fended off the question with a raise of his hand. 'Nothing, just a little surprise that's all. Come on, follow me.'

He stopped at the door to the boat yard. 'Now, both of you close your eyes.'

'What on earth for?' asked his wife, giving him an impatient look.

'Humour me, please.'

Carol looked at Gemma and shrugged. 'OK, Bob Lewis, but it better be good. You've taken me away from making a complicated necklace and you know how much I hate leaving when I'm in the middle of working on something.'

'Just close your eyes Carol and it will soon be over.' He looked across at his daughter. 'You too, Gemma.'

Both women obediently closed their eyes. Gemma felt her father take her hand and pull both of them towards the door.

'Mind the step,' he said as he guided them inside the building and told them to halt. 'OK, open your eyes.'

Both women stared in front of them. The campervan stood in all its glory, a large red ribbon tied around its middle with a sign hanging from the bow. In large black letters was written 'Carol's Cruiser'.

'Well, what do you think?' asked Bob as both women stood in silence looking at the sight in front of them.

'Love the name,' said Gemma looking over at her mother who appeared to be speechless.

'Well, I was going to do a bit of sign writing and put it on the side but I thought that maybe that was a step too far for your mother.'

'You've finished it,' stated Carol, still staring at the campervan.

'I have indeed, and to mark the occasion I thought we'd have a 'cutting of the ribbon' ceremony.' He produced a pair of scissors from his pocket. 'Care to do the honours?' he said passing them to Carol.

'I can't believe after all these months it's actually finished,' Carol said, standing in front of the large bow and looking over the van before her eyes rested on the sign. 'Yes, maybe a step too far.' She gave her husband a smile. 'I name this land yacht 'Carol's Cruiser', may all who travel in her have a safe journey.'

Both Bob and Gemma clapped as the ribbon was cut.

'So, I was thinking,' said Bob. 'How about you and me going on a little test run at the weekend? I can check out how it drives and you can get acquainted with the cooker.'

'Always thinking of your stomach,' said Carol, shaking her head at her husband. 'But why not, sounds like a good idea.' She turned to her daughter. 'Are you OK with that? You don't need us to stay for anything?'

'Of course not. You go off and enjoy yourselves. With any luck Penny will have turned up by the end of the week and I'll be back in London.'

'Let's hope so.' She turned back to Bob. 'So where do you plan on taking me on this little trip?'

Bob scratch at his chin. 'To be honest I hadn't really thought it out. How about we just turn the engine on and see where the steering wheel leads us.'

'Sounds great. Come on, let's check out the inside. See what we need to take with us.'

Gemma watched her parents headed

towards their mobile home. Her mother giggled at something her father said. She felt a flash of envy wishing she could have just a little of the magic her parents radiated. Maybe, one day, she thought wistfully. She pulled out her mobile — still no message from Dan. What was he up to?

* * *

Gemma closed her sketch pad and rubbed tired eyes. The afternoon had faded into night and there was still no word from Dan even though she'd texted him several times and rung his number. The texts were unanswered and the phone went straight to answer. She'd even contemplated going back to the folly to see if she could search out any further clues, but stupidly she'd voiced her intentions and her father gave her a stern warning not to even think about doing something on her own.

She opened her sketch book again.

She was working on the drawings for a new client. The author forwarded a copy of the book just before Gemma left London and she'd promised to have some rough sketches for approval as soon as possible. The story was about a family of seagulls with a mischievous youngster called Sammy who was born with a wonky beak that made it difficult for him to eat. Gemma enjoyed creating the character with his wide, innocent eyes, and the slightly twisted beak. She ran a finger along the outline of his body — she was pleased with what she saw on paper. At least her work world was looking up, even if her personal life seemed to be in a turmoil at the moment.

She checked her watch, surprised to see that it was past midnight. When she was working the hours seemed to slip as she delved herself in the world of her characters. She remembered her mother calling out goodnight. She closed her eyes and let the quiet of the house surround her only to be suddenly interrupted by the sound of her phone ringing.

At last. She picked up her phone. Dan was about to get a piece of her mind.

16

Gemma tapped her fingers on the steering wheel. It was early morning and once again she waiting outside the train station for Dan. She was frustrated at their conversation on the telephone the night before. He'd been full of apologies about not including her in the trip but he'd wanted to get off early in the morning and didn't want to wake her.

'A poor excuse,' she'd managed to interject before he also apologised for not returning her calls but he'd turned off his mobile at one point and forgot to turn it back on. She wasn't quite convinced if that was the truth but decided not to enquire further. His next words took her by surprise, though.

'We need to check out Westlea Manor.'

'Why?'

'I'll explain when I get back. Can you pick me up at the station tomorrow morning at seven o'clock?' His voice was brisk and before she could ask any more questions he said a quick goodbye, leaving Gemma none the wiser and a little more irritated.

Right on time she saw him emerge from the entrance clutching a cup of coffee in his hand.

'Well?' she said once he'd settled himself into his seat. 'Do I get a better explanation about yesterday, Dan?'

He looked at her for a moment. He must have seen the anger flashing in her eyes. He raised one of his hands in defence. 'OK, OK. I'm sorry. I didn't think it would be that much of an issue.'

'Exactly. You didn't think.' She took a deep breath trying to control her temper.

'Look, Gemma, you have to understand. I'm used to being in control. It's how I am. For a long time now I've never answered to anyone. I went on a hunch. I left you out of the mix. I promise not to do it again.' He looked at her with those piercing blue eyes that made her forgive him anything. 'Am I forgiven?'

She looked at him for a moment and felt her temper begin to cool as she noticed, for the first time, the dark circles under his eyes and the worry lines crossing his brow.

'I'll think about it.' He wasn't getting off the hook that easily. She turned the engine on and headed out of the station. 'So, are you going to tell me what you found out yesterday?'

Dan took a gulp of coffee before answering her. 'As I said to you the other day, it's all about following the money. I couldn't get it out of my head how Tovey managed to purchase the Manor after being made bankrupt.'

'Thought we decided he could have put some by for a rainy day.'

'Yes, that's the conclusion I first came to but after thinking about it some more I wasn't so sure. I was still convinced that there was someone else involved.'

'And you found someone?'

'No, but I called a friend of mine who works on one of the national papers to check out Tovey's previous business.'

'But you already did that on the internet. Surely all the information you needed was there?'

'Not all, no. There's always some bits of information that get hidden away.'

'So what did you find out?'

'Well, there was no offshore account. No money hidden away. When he lost his business he was completely broke. Nothing left. Not one penny. Apparently Henderson was right when he said he had no brains. Anyway, according to my mate, he disappeared for a couple of years and then he's suddenly turned up with enough money to put a deposit on the Manor and charm the local council with promises of updating the place.'

'So we're no further forward?'

'Oh, I wouldn't say that. I think we'll

find our answer at the Manor. I also think we'll get closer to finding Brian and Penny.' He looked across at her. 'Gemma, I think the puzzle is coming together. Just a few more pieces to find.'

'I hope so, Dan. I'm not sure I can take much more of this.'

'Only a little longer. Be patient.'

He finished his coffee. 'Now, how far is this other entrance?'

'We have to drive past the Manor and there's an old road that takes us to the stable block. Well, when I say old road, it's more like a cinder track. It's still used by ramblers as a short cut to the cliffs. The colonel allowed the access because it was out of sight of the manor house and he was never disturbed.'

'Perfect.'

The roads were beginning to fill with early morning traffic as Gemma steered the car out of Westlea and headed inland.

'So, did you find out anything else of interest about Tovey?'

'Yes, a bit of personal info which was

interesting,' Dan answered mysteriously.

'Interesting. How?'

'He's the second child of John and Margaret Tovey. His parents were killed in a car crash when he was ten. He went to live with an elderly relative. A big insurance payment from his parent's accident ensured that he could go to private school, which was probably for the best, as the guardian had little interest in him. Most likely why he went off the rails at school.'

'Why's that?'

'For attention.'

'Yes, I can see that. But back track a minute. You said there was the second child. So there was a sibling. What happened to them?'

'Mm. That's where the info sort of runs a bit dry. My mate tried to dig a bit more but could only find out that there was a few years difference in age between the two children. Anyway, the elder one, a girl, didn't get on with the parents. The usual teenage stuff. Didn't like the rules of the house, so left home. Disappeared into the mists of runaways and hasn't been heard of since.'

'What was her name?' Gemma enquired.

'Edith, I believe. Why?'

Gemma shrugged. 'Just wondered. But you say that Tovey was left some insurance money. Maybe that's what helped him purchase the manor house?'

'That was my thought but it wasn't the case. After paying for his private education there was very little left. Certainly not enough to put a deposit down on a large country pile.'

Gemma took a turning onto a country lane. 'It's just up ahead.'

She pulled onto the grass verge and parked behind a tall hedgerow. 'It's best we leave the car here and walk. We don't want to be spotted,' she said, turning off the engine.

'Good idea. Is this the track you were talking about?' said Dan as he stepped out of the car and nodded towards a dirt track in front of them which meandered downwards and around a cluster of trees to the left before disappearing from view.

'Yes,' she said, heading towards it. 'The house won't come into view until we pass the trees. There's a stable block to the side of the house, although in the Colonel's day it was converted into garage space and accommodation above for the housekeeper.'

'Didn't you say this track was only used by ramblers?' said Dan.

'Yes. Why?'

'Well, unless they've stopped using their feet and are rambling in vehicles I'd say something else has used this road recently. Look, there are tyre tracks.'

Dan was right and it looked as though the tracks were fresh, the indents left in the earth.

'Perhaps Tovey is using this road to have materials for the refurbishment delivered?'

'Maybe, but for some reason, I doubt it.'

They followed the track down and around the trees until the buildings came into view. There was a SUV parked outside the stable block.

'Looks like we've lucked out,' said Gemma. 'The master of the house is at home. So what do we do now?'

She looked over at Dan.

'I have an idea,' he said, reaching into his pocket for his phone. She watched as he dialled a number.

She frowned and was about to ask him a question when he raised a finger to stop her.

'Hello,' he said, after a moment. 'I've just seen some kids playing outside the folly at Westlea Manor. There's a sign outside saying the place is dangerous. Think the owner ought to know. Right. Yes. Thanks. Goodbye.'

He disconnected, put the phone back in his pocket and looked at Gemma. 'Now, we wait.'

Gemma admired his inventiveness and it wasn't until much later that she wondered why she didn't ask him how he knew the number of the local police station. She turned to watch if anything was going to happen. She didn't have to wait long. A few moments later, a door to the stable block opened and she could see Tovey, quickly followed by Norton, shrugging on jackets and running in the direction of the folly.

'Well that worked out well,' he said, grinning at Gemma. 'Come on. Hopefully the diversion should keep them busy for a while,' said Dan, his blue eyes sparkling and a grin on his face. He reached out and caught Gemma's hand and began jogging towards the stable block.

'Let's see if we can check out what's inside.'

They approached two large double doors at the front of the building. He twisted the handle and pulled the door open to reveal an area large enough to hold at least three or four cars, although there was only one in residence.

'Well, it looks as though we've solved the mystery of Brian's car,' he said, walking over to the vehicle he clearly recognised. He peered inside but the car was empty.

'How about the boot?' said Gemma, although if she was honest with herself she'd rather not know if there was anything unpleasant inside. Dan must have sensed her unease. He reached out, taking her hand and gave it a squeeze of reassurance before moving to the back of the car. He hesitated for a second and Gemma knew that he was feeling the same nerves as herself. She watched him take a deep breath before releasing the catch and pulling open the lid. He looked inside for a moment saying nothing before she watched his shoulders relax.

'Empty,' he said and she felt the breath she was holding whoosh out of her.

Dan shut the lid. 'Come on. Let's check out the main house. We might not have much time before Tovey and Norton return.' He pulled her outside and shut the garage doors.

She walked towards the main house before she glanced back to find Dan on his mobile phone and few yards behind her.

'I thought you were in a hurry. Now is not the time to make a phone call.' When this was all over she was going to find out the problem with Dan and his phone, but now wasn't the time.

'Sorry,' he said, pocketing his mobile, saying nothing about whoever he was calling.

They passed the old kitchen garden and walked over the courtyard towards the kitchen entrance.

Gemma twisted the handle but it wouldn't budge an inch.

'Here, let me,' said Dan. Reaching around her, gripping the knob, he gave it a strong twist and pushed. The door opened with the sound of creaking wood.

'Doesn't look as though this entrance has been used for some time,' he said. 'Come on, let's see what we can discover.' He rested a hand against the middle of Gemma's back and pushed her inside.

The kitchen was in a sad state of repair. Cupboards covered the walls, many with doors missing or hanging from broken hinges. The appliances were old and in some cases rusted with age. No attempt had been made to update the room into a functioning kitchen.

'Come on. We might not have much time. Let's check out the rest of the house.'

Gemma gave the kitchen one more glance before following Dan. The rooms were much the same as the kitchen. Anything of value was long gone. The walls showed signs of pictures that once hung in splendour. Much of the decorative coving edging the high ceilings was broken, large pieces lying on the floor. The debris showing echoes of the past.

'This is so sad,' she said, as she followed Dan from one room to another.

Dan nodded.

'Well nothing down here,' he said after they inspected the last room. 'Let's see what we can find on the next level.'

Gemma followed him up the once grand staircase and moved along the corridor, opening doors and checking the rooms. Every one empty.

'Well, that's the last one,' said Dan, closing the final door. 'Anywhere else you can think of?'

He sounded defeated. Gemma felt the same. She was sure they would find Brian and Penny in the house.

'We could try the attic, I suppose,' she said after a moment.

'Any idea how we find an entrance?'

Gemma shook her head. 'No idea, but I should imagine it's somewhere along here.'

They headed back along the corridor, opening all the doors once again but still they could find an access.

'Nothing,' said Gemma, trying to keep the disappointment from her voice.

'Oh, I don't know,' said Dan moving

past her. 'What's through here?'

She turned to see a tiny entrance tucked away in the corner.

'Think we've found it. There's stone steps leading upwards. Come on.' He didn't wait but disappeared up the stairs. Gemma quickly followed, climbing the twisting staircase until she almost bumped into Dan when he stopped at the top. A long corridor lay in front of them with several doors to one side.

'I always thought an attic was one big room,' said Dan, heading towards the first door.

'Not in the Victorian era. These rooms would have been used for the servants' quarters.'

'Oh, of course.' He twisted the door handle and it turned easily but looking inside, there was nothing there.

Gemma walked along the corridor and tried the next door. It was locked but she was sure she heard a noise.

'Dan. Over here. I think there's someone inside.' She tried to keep the excitement out of her voice and she watched Dan put his ear to the door to listen.

'Brian, is that you?' he called. A muffled sound came from the room. 'It's him.' He twisted the door knob but it didn't budge. He gave it a shove with his shoulder — but still nothing.

'I need something to break it down.'

They both looked around the corridor but there was nothing.

'Hang on a minute,' said Gemma, seeing something along the top of the door frame. She reached up, running her hands along the narrow rim before making contact with cold metal.

She smiled. 'This do?' In her hand was a large, gold key.

'Can't believe it was left there.'

'Safest place, I suppose,' said Gemma as Dan inserted the key and unlocked the door.

The missing couple were sitting in the corner of the room, arms wrapped around each other, looking tired and scared.

'Thank goodness you've found us,' cried Penny and Gemma ran across the room to her friend.

'You OK?' asked Gemma, pulling Penny's trembling body into a hug.

'Better now I've seen you,' said Penny.

'You got my phone call, then?' said Brian, standing up and looking at Dan.

Gemma looked across at Dan. What phone call? He gave her a quick glance but said nothing before turning to Brian.

'Come on,' said Dan, hurrying towards the door. 'Let's get out of this place. There will be time for explanations later.'

Gemma stood still for a moment. What was going on? It was obvious that Dan knew more than he'd originally told her.

'Where's Tovey and Norton?' asked Brian, as the small group made their escape. He looked down the corridor as though he was expecting their captors to appear at any moment.

'Hopefully still on a wild goose chase,' remarked Dan with a smile.

They hurried along the corridor and down the staircase, Dan leading the way. They were in the last corridor leading into the kitchen when Norton appeared in front of them, a gun in his hand, Tovey beside him.

'Well, well, well,' Tovey said, a smirk crossing his face as he looked at Dan. 'Not content in trying to gain entrance to the folly, now you're taking a look at my home without an invitation. I see you've found my other guests.'

'We're no guests of yours,' said Brian, taking a step forward. Dan reached out a hand to restrain his brother.

'Very wise,' said Tovey. 'Sorry, I can't offer you tea but I'm a bit busy at the moment.' He began to turn then halted and looked directly at Dan. 'You really shouldn't have interfered.' He turned to Norton. 'Take their mobiles, then lock them up. We'll deal with them later.' Without another word he walked out of the kitchen.

Norton quickly removed Dan and Gemma's mobiles and waggled the gun at them. 'Come on, back to the penthouse suite,' he said, laughing at his own bad taste joke.

Dan reached out to Gemma and laced his fingers through hers. She tried to pull away from him, still angry about whatever he'd concealed from her. His fingers tightened around her own and before she could say anything Norton was pushing against Dan's strong shoulders urging him forward.

She could hear the sound of Penny sobbing behind and Brian trying to reassure her. Dan said nothing, just kept on walking. They were in a mess.

The lock turning in the door and the sound of fading footsteps made Penny cry even louder and Gemma went over to comfort her friend.

Dan scrubbed a hand over his face before running his fingers through his hair. 'OK, Brian. Care to tell us what's going on?'

'You got my phone call. I explained everything.'

'Yes, I got your phone call. Or at least, I got a very garbled message when I landed at Heathrow. Something about Westlea Bay, drugs and smuggling and Justin Price. Nothing else made sense.'

'You knew,' said Gemma, her voice rising. 'All this time, and you knew what was going on?'

Those piercing blue eyes locked with hers for a moment. 'Let Brian tell his story then I'll explain.'

'OK, but it better be good.' She wanted to know his side of the story but before that it was obvious Dan needed to hear his brother's tale.

Brian sighed. 'I was doing my usual call at Bradshaw's a few months ago. He was out so that girl, Hayley, told me to wait in his office. His desk was covered in all kinds of drugs. Not unusual for a chemist, but what caught my eye was the packaging.'

'What was wrong with the packaging?' asked Gemma, looking puzzled.

'It was all in a foreign language and not, as I had expected, written in English. Anyway, I'd just picked up a box to examine in when Bradshaw walked in. He snatched the box out of my hand and started ranting on about me being nosy. Of course, I asked him what he was up to. It didn't take long for him to tell me about fake prescription drugs being smuggled in from abroad. How he could distribute them through his connections on the market stalls he'd worked on years ago.'

'Ah, so that ship out in the bay does have something to do with it,' said Dan.

'Oh, so you've found out about that then?'

Dan nodded.

'I didn't do anything about it to start off with. I hoped that I could persuade him to stop his activities. My mistake. Over the next few visits I pressed him further about who was involved. He was reluctant at first but I wasn't going to give up. There's nothing worse than putting unsafe drugs out into the market place for the general public to purchase.

'There was a gang of them. Mates from his school days. One of them, Tovey, knew about this old smugglers' passageway at Westlea Manor. The place was up for sale and he'd bought it for the sole purpose of their little venture. On every visit he tried to get me to join them.' Brian gave a look of pure disgust at the thought. 'Of course I told him I wasn't interested. In the end I knew he wasn't going to change his mind, so told him I was going to the police.'

'So why didn't you?'

'I was going to but needed to talk to Penny first. I hadn't told her any of it. I also knew you were on your way home and if anything happened to us you would go to the police. I left that message on your phone as I hurried home.'

Penny sniffed and took a deep breath before taking up the story. 'I knew as soon as Brian told me we were in

293

trouble. Tovey and Norton arrived later that night, threatening us. I was talking to you on the phone in the kitchen but I heard shouting. Brian saying he was going to the police. The next thing I heard was something about taking us to Westlea Manor.' Penny paused for a moment, wringing her hands. 'Anyway, I was having to think on my feet and mentioned the folly to you, hoping that you'd see through the little white lie I told.'

'Well, thankfully it worked,' said Gemma.

'So sorry to have got you mixed up in this.' She began to cry again.

'So, did you manage to get hold of Justin Price?' Brian said to his brother.

'Who's Justin Price?' asked Gemma. She stared at Dan, her arms crossed. 'I think it's about time you told me the whole truth.'

17

Dan watched as Gemma bit down on her lip. She was staring at him, a mixture of anger and hurt showing on her face.

Running a hand through his hair he paced the room, saying nothing.

'Well, I'm waiting.'

'OK.' Dan looked directly at Gemma, his eyes never leaving her face as he began to talk.

'My plane landed much earlier in the day and when I picked up Brian's garbled message I dashed home.'

'You mean you arrived at Brian's house before I did?'

Dan nodded.

'I knew something was wrong as soon as I walked into the house. Brian's message mentioned Justin Price. He's an old school friend who works for the fraud squad. I called him.'

'The fraud squad knows?' said Gemma, interrupting Dan.

He held up a hand. 'Just let me finish Gemma, please. It's hard enough as it is.'

He knew she wanted to ask questions and he was sure the list would grow as he told his tale.

'I phoned Justin and arranged to meet him. After he listened to Brian's message he told me that Tovey was under suspicion by the fraud squad, but they needed proof. He asked if I could help them.'

'Why didn't you say?'

He shrugged. 'I thought maybe you were involved. I thought Penny might be involved as well,' he admitted.

'Me?' said Penny, who started crying again making Brian glare at his brother and pull Penny closer to him, whispering words of comfort.

'Sorry, Penny, but to be honest we'd never met and it was a possibility.'

'And what about me?' said Gemma.

'I wanted to find out if you knew

anything. When you mentioned the folly and how it was not a favourite place of Penny's, I knew that it must be a clue. I've been reporting back every day since we met.'

'Did you ever trust me?' said Gemma, her voice void of emotion.

He reached out to touch her but she stepped back avoiding the connection.

'It didn't take me long to realise that you weren't involved. I kept quiet because Justin asked me too. He thought it would be safer if you were none the wiser.'

'Any other reason?'

Dan sighed. 'You're headstrong, Gemma. That's one of the things I like about you. If you knew everything you would have gone straight to Tovey to try to get him to admit all. It would have put you in danger. I'm not sorry I didn't tell you. I just couldn't let anything happen to you.' He watched her shoulders relax a little and hoped he was getting through to her.

'There was also another reason,' he continued. 'Justin indicated that there was someone else involved. They knew about Tovey, Norton and Bradshaw, but were certain that there was someone higher up.'

'The money person?' said Gemma.

'Exactly.'

'So the numerous phone calls and trips to London. You were doing what?'

'Reporting back. Checking facts with Justin.'

He watched Gemma as she paced across the room, back and forth, absorbing everything he'd revealed to her. After a couple of lengths of the room she stopped and turned to him.

'So have you found out who else is involved?'

'Yes.'

'Who is . . . ' began Gemma but the sound of the door unlocking halted her question. Norton stood there, gun in hand and a sneer on his face.

'OK, folks. Time to get moving.' The gun twitched in his hand as he indicated for them to move towards the door.

'Where are we going?' asked Brian as he led a calmer Penny down the stairs.

'You'll find out soon enough,' said Norton, pushing the gun into Brian's back.

Entering the kitchen, Tovey was waiting for them with someone else Gemma recognised.

'Whitey?'

The friendly landlady Gemma had known for years was gone. In her place a cold eyed woman who did not look happy.

'Hello dearie,' she said, walking towards them. 'Surprised to see me?' She didn't wait for a reply but carried on talking. 'You couldn't leave it alone, could you? I knew you were up to something the minute you brought your friend here,' she nodded towards Dan, 'to the hotel and told me you wanted to check out the folly. Then he kept disappearing back to London when he was supposed to be looking around the area and architecture. Roused my suspicions that the pair of you were up to something. Didn't take me long to realise that you were looking for your friend here.' She looked over at Penny who instinctively huddled to Brian's side. 'If that ship hadn't broken down, they would have been long gone and you'd never have found them.'

'I can't believe this. Why? How?' Gemma looked at Whitey, the shock showing on her face.

The laugh Whitey gave wasn't pleasant. 'Well, I suppose I better give you some sort of explanation before you head out to sea for the short cruise you're going to take.'

Penny let out a loud wail. 'We're all going to die, aren't we?'

Ignoring the interruption, Whitey continued. 'Meet Hugo Tovey. My brother.'

'Your brother?' said Gemma, glancing at Dan who nodded. 'You're the sister who disappeared?'

'Ah, I see you've been checking up on me. Let's not go through the family history, suffice to say that after many years apart we found each other. We both discovered we were struggling with a cash flow problem. I came up with the idea of smuggling. Lucrative to say the least.'

'But how did you know about the folly and the hidden passage?'

'Comes from being nosy when I lived here as a teenager. Went exploring in the loft one day and came across a diary, detailing its existence. The chap who built this pile discovered it when he bought the place and built the folly over the entrance.'

'But why, Whitey? I don't understand. You seemed happy running The Ship.'

Whitey gave out a laugh. 'Happy. No, I've never been happy there. Waiting on other people. You must be joking.'

'The travel brochures. They weren't for a guest, were they?'

'No. I'm taking a little trip. Off to San Francisco. There's still a hippy community there. I'm going to disappear. Hugo can run the business while I retire and just take my cut.'

'It seems like you've got it all sown up,' growled Dan.

'You could say that, although there were a couple of problems.'

'Oh yes, and what were they?'

'Nosy parker, here.' She pointed to Brian. 'If only he would have agreed to come on board with us, nobody would have been the wiser.'

'I would never have gone along with your plan,' said Brian, his face red with anger.

'Pity. Now, because of your honesty, you've involved your girlfriend, Gemma and Dan. Who are you by the way? Police?' She looked over at Dan who said nothing.

'He's my brother,' said Brian when the silence increased.'

'Nice little family unit, wouldn't you say, Edith?' said Tovey.

Whitey looked over at her brother and grinned. 'Well, at least they'll go together.' The grin vanished and she was immediately back to business. 'OK,

Bradshaw should be at the folly by now. Let's get going.'

The group headed out, followed by Norton.

'Walk them up,' Tovey instructed. 'We'll follow in the car.'

Whitey and Tovey held back for a moment, speaking in whispers.

Dusk was falling. Penny began to cry again.

Gemma reached out and touched her arm. 'It's going to be all right.'

Penny sniffed and gave her a watery smile. 'Sorry to have got you into this mess, Gemma.'

'Hey, just think of it as an adventure. Wherever it leads us, we'll be fine.' Reassuring words, but Gemma was unsure if they were the truth because at the moment she couldn't see how they were getting out of the mess.

She stumbled a couple of times and Dan reached out and took her hand.

'Any ideas?' she whispered as they trudged up the hill that lead to the folly.

'Thinking about it,' he said but didn't elaborate.

Before she could quiz him further the folly came into view and she could see Bradshaw waiting for them. He was not alone. The two foreign sailors stood beside him.

'Looks like we have an escort.'

Dan's mouth was set in a grim line. 'Yes, looks like it.'

Suddenly as they neared Bradshaw, Penny let go of Brian's hand and launched herself at her old boss.

'How could you?' she screamed at him, as she punched him in the chest.

'Get off me woman,' he said, shoving her away with more force than was necessary, causing her to stumble and fall to the ground.

'Leave her alone,' said Brian, running towards Bradshaw, his fists clenched ready to hit out at the older man. One of the sailors quickly stepped in and held Brian back as Dan shouted to his brother to stop.

In the commotion nobody noticed

Tovey's car pull up.

'OK, folks. Break it up,' said Whitey as she stepped out of the car and walked towards them.

Brian helped Penny to her feet and pulled her to his side. 'What's going to happen to us now?'

'A little cruise, although you'll be getting your feet wet before you get to dry land,' said Whitey.

Norton laughed nastily. 'Yeah, and there'll be no life jackets.'

Gemma look across at Dan but he was looking past her towards the trees in the distance. She hoped he was looking for an escape route.

She turned to Whitey. 'It's not too late. Let us go and we'll say nothing.'

'You should've thought about your safety before you started interfering. Now you'll pay.' She paused for a moment and Gemma thought she might be changing her mind. 'I'm sorry it had to end this way. I'll make sure I comfort your parents when they hear of your demise.'

Gemma bit down on her lip and held back the angry words she wanted to bestow on the woman she once thought of so fondly. She didn't even want to think about her parents and how they would handle their loss.

'OK, enough talking.' Whitey looked over at her brother. 'Let's get moving.'

'Right, this way ladies and gentlemen,' said Norton, nudging his gun sharply into Dan's side.

Gemma watched Dan, a little disappointed that he didn't resist but he, once again, seemed to be looking out into the distance. What on earth was he looking for? The answer came soon enough. As she stepped onto the first steps of the folly the sound of police sirens could be heard. Looking up she saw the flashing lights of police cars racing down the road before turning towards the folly.

'Cops,' shouted Bradshaw, running in the opposite direction to the oncoming cars.

Chaos followed. The two sailors

turned towards the entrance of the folly and quickly went inside. Norton began running down the hill, firing bullets at the police cars. He threw the gun to the ground once the chamber was empty. With nowhere to go the police apprehended him. Whitey must have realised that the game was up and just stood there, a resigned look on her face.

In all the confusion, Gemma couldn't see Tovey.

She turned to Dan but he was running towards the cliff top, Tovey just ahead of him trying another escape route. Running after them she saw Dan catching hold of Tovey's arm as he neared the cliff edge before the other man shrugged him off. To her horror, he produced a gun and pointed it at Dan.

No way, thought Gemma as she came up beside the pair and launched herself at Tovey. She heard Dan shout her name. Tovey tried to push her away but she managed to catch the hand that held the gun. She heard the sound of the gun firing. Tovey fell to the ground, pulling Gemma on top of him. She pulled herself free and saw a pool of blood seeping through a wound in Tovey's shoulder. She looked round to assure Dan she was OK but he wasn't there.

'Dan,' she screamed out in sheer panic.

'Down here,' he called from somewhere beyond the cliff. Without a second thought of her fear of cliff edges she followed the sound of his voice. She looked over the cliff edge. Dan was clinging to the thick branch of a bush. She could see blood running from a nasty gash to his forehead. He was struggling to get a foot hold without much success. The memory of her childhood nightmare flashed through her mind. It was now all too real. She pushed away the thought. She lay down flat on her stomach. Dan needed her help.

'Grab hold of my hand, Dan,' she

said, shifting as close to the cliff edge as she dared, reaching out her hand. 'Get some leverage with your feet.'

'Think I've broken my ankle. Too painful.'

'Try using your elbows, then,' she suggested.

Dan moved a little and let go, trying to capture her hand but it was just out of reach.

'It's no good, Gemma,' he shouted.

Gemma edged a little further, her body almost falling over the cliff top.

'Come on, Dan. Try harder.'

Another attempt and still Dan couldn't reach.

Gemma checked her position, if she went further she would topple over herself. The next effort would have to come from Dan. She eased herself forward a fraction of an inch.

'OK, this time,' she said, through gritted teeth. 'You'd better make it a real good effort because I'm still waiting for a big apology from you for keeping things from me, and believe me

I'm going to enjoy every humble word you say.'

Despite the danger he was in, Dan chuckled.

She watched as he reached out for her one more time, his face straining with effort. She felt his fingertips touch hers and, with an extra push, he finally locked onto her outstretched hand.

'OK, I've got you,' she said, her breath raspy from exerting the energy to hold onto him. She felt his hand begin to slip out of her own and she tried to hang on.

'Let me go, Gemma,' he said.

She looked down at those piercing blue eyes and knew it wouldn't happen.

'Never,' she whispered. She gripped onto his fingers until she managed to get a better hold and began to pull with all her strength. A dead weight is not easy to pull and try as she might she was making very little headway.

She heard someone running towards her. A quick look over her shoulder and she saw Justin Price kneel down beside her and reach out for Dan's hand.

'It's OK, I've got him,' he said, pulling Dan to safety with ease.

Gemma heaved a sigh of relief. Dan was safe. She wrapped her arms around him.

'I thought I'd lost you,' she whispered.

'Not a chance,' replied Dan with a weak smile, as Justin checked he was OK before returning to the chaos behind them.

Gemma looked down at the folly. Whitey and her accomplices were being put in a police van. An ambulance had arrived and she watched as medics led Brian and Penny towards it.

It was all over. She wondered where it left her and Dan's relationship.

18

Two hours later, Gemma was sitting on an uncomfortable plastic chair, a cup of warm coffee in her hand waiting to see Dan. His ankle was indeed broken and a cast applied. The gash on his head was deep enough to warrant a few stitches but overall he was all right. She closed her eyes and leant back, her head resting on the wall. She was tired but her mind kept going over the events of the last few days.

Justin Price spoke to her after his visit with Dan, apologising for keeping her in the dark but emphasising that it was in her best interests. In the cold light of day he was probably right.

Penny was reunited with her father, who was a little shell-shocked to find out for the first time that his daughter had been in danger for the past few days. He couldn't stop thanking Brian for taking care of his only child. It looked as though the family were, at last, united.

Gemma phoned her parents, relating the events of the day. She assured them she was fine and not to worry.

The door to the side ward opened and a nurse walked out.

'You can see him now,' she said. 'We're keeping him overnight for observation but then he can go home.'

Gemma thanked her and headed into the room.

Dan lay on the bed, his ankle in a white cast; a large plaster covered the stitches on his forehead.

He was checking something on his phone but placed it on the night stand as the door opened. Those blue eyes locked on hers as she walked up to his bedside and before he could say anything she spoke first.

'OK. Explain away,' she said, trying to sound angry although she couldn't quite pull it off.

'Am I forgiven?' he said, sitting

upright in bed, ignoring her words.

Her lips moved in a half smile. 'Depends on what you tell me.'

He gave out a huge sigh and leant back again the pillow, closing his eyes.

'Well, you know most of it. I'm sorry I didn't tell you but Brian's my brother, my only relative. His safety comes first.'

She could understand that and nodded. 'I recognised your friend Justin. He was the man you were talking to at the station and then he popped up in Brighton.'

'I had to think on my feet when you saw him that morning. He'd come down to see for himself what was going on.'

Gemma pulled up a chair and sat down. 'What I don't understand is how you suspected Whitey.'

Dan reached out and linked his hand with hers. She didn't pull away.

'It came to me gradually. The first clue was the bells she wore round her neck.'

Gemma looked at him in surprise. Of

all the things she'd expected him to say, that wasn't one of them.

'I heard the sound of the chimes one night when I was outside The Ship. It was just after I heard someone talking to Bradshaw. Then I heard them again when we were eating there.'

'What else?'

'Remember the travel brochures?'

Gemma nodded.

'She lied. They were never for a guest but for herself. A trip she was never going to return from . . . '

'There must be more to it than the sound of bells and a couple of travel brochures?'

'There is. To be honest I wasn't sure if I was on the right track but Justin was pushing me to find some answers. As you know they knew of Tovey and the others, but still felt there was someone else involved. The police wanted to catch all the culprits, leaving nothing to resolve.' He paused for a moment and reached for a glass of water on the cabinet by his bed.

'I remembered Whitey telling me about her childhood one night. She mentioned the village where she grew up. I knew I'd heard that name before and when I checked it was near the private school Tovey attended. He came from the same village. After his sister disappeared his parents wanted him to attend a school near them, so I went to London to meet Justin.' A grin swept across his face. 'It's easy to find out details when you have the police on your side. Birth certificates proved that Whitey, or should I say Edith, was the sister of Tovey. After that information everything seemed to fall into place.' He gave a deep sigh. 'And that's about it . . . '

Gemma raised an eyebrow. 'Not quite. One more question.'

'Fire away,' he said and Gemma cringed at his choice of words, remembering the bullet that entered Tovey's shoulder.

'How did the police know where to find us?'

'Ah. Yes, well remember you caught me using my phone after we found Brian's car? I was sending Justin a signal. We'd agreed that they wouldn't make a move until two things happened.'

'Two things?'

'We found Brian and Penny and Whitey would make an appearance. We felt sure that would happen because the ship out in the bay was repaired and ready to head out to sea.'

'So that's why you were looking over your shoulder. You were checking to see where the police were?'

Dan nodded. 'They followed Bradshaw. Waited just off the main road. Justin told me they waited until the whole gang were together before they made their move. Thank goodness no one was seriously hurt when Norton started shooting.'

Gemma's head was buzzing. She was sure she had more questions to ask, but she'd heard enough for the moment. She felt Dan squeeze her fingers.

'I asked you a question when you walked into the room. I'll ask you again. Am I forgiven?'

She looked down at their hands entwined and then into his eyes and saw the sincerity there.

'I almost lost you.' Her voice trembled and she felt a tear slide down her cheek.

'But you didn't,' said Dan, reaching out and thumbing the tear away. 'Now are you going to answer my question?'

'You're forgiven,' she said, a smile spreading across her features.

She hadn't noticed how tense he'd been while waiting for her answer. He sighed with relief, his shoulders relaxing as he pulled her towards him.

'I love you, Gemma,' he confessed.

'You do?'

'You were about to sacrifice your life to try and save mine. I could have pulled you off that cliff.' He shuddered at the thought.

'I couldn't let you go,' she murmured. 'That's when I realised I love you, too.'

318

Dan's face broke out into a smile. 'Hop up,' he said, patting the bed.

'What about your ankle?'

'Never mind my ankle. I need to hold you.'

Gemma gave a token protest but Dan pulled her onto the bed and wrapped his strong arms around her. 'We've been on quite an adventure, haven't we?'

'We have indeed.'

'Hopefully we'll have many more.'

'Can we get over this one first?'

'All right, but let's not leave it too long. There are places I want to take you to. Sights to see. Who knows what we will find on our travels.'

She looked into those piercing blue eyes. She could see sincerity and love. He would keep her safe. She reached up and touched his cheek. 'Can it wait until you kiss me?'

Before he could answer, his mobile rang.

Gemma rolled her eyes. 'Don't you dare answer it.'

'Wouldn't dream of it,' he whispered as his arms tightened around her and he brought his lips down to meet hers.

FLEUR DE CORSE

Wendy Kremer

Catrin confronts a man trespassing on her Aunt Hazel's land, only to learn that he is Hazel's godson, Alex. He's a successful architect, handsome but irritating — and when he offers to buy Hazel's property, Catrin is immediately suspicious. Can she trust his motives, or does he have something to gain from the arrangement? Accompanying Hazel on a trip to Corsica, Catrin ponders this — but when Alex turns up unexpectedly, her feelings begin to change. Still, she's determined to uncover his true intentions for her aunt's land . . .